LEAVING
HOME

Anita Brookner

LEAVING HOME

A Novel

RANDOM HOUSE

NEW YORK

Copyright © 2005 by Anita Brookner

Published in the United States by Random House, an imprint
of The Random House Publishing Group,
a division of Random House, Inc., New York.

RANDOM HOUSE and colophon are registered
trademarks of Random House, Inc.

This work was originally published in hardcover in the
United Kingdom by Viking, an imprint
of Penguin Books, a member of the Penguin Group, in 2005.

LIBRARY OF CONGRESS CATALOGING-IN-PUBLICATION DATA
Brookner, Anita.
Leaving home: a novel / Anita Brookner.
p.   cm.
ISBN 1-4000-6414-7
1. Young women—Fiction. 2. Mothers and daughters—Fiction. 3. Female friendship—
Fiction. 4. British—France—Fiction. 5. Mothers—Death—Fiction. 6. London
(England)—Fiction. 7. Women scholars—Fiction. 8. France—Fiction. I. Title.
PR6052.R5816L43 2006   822'.914—dc22   2005048957

Printed in the United States of America on acid-free paper

www.atrandom.com

2 4 6 8 9 7 5 3 1

First U.S. Edition

Book design by Victoria Wong

LEAVING
HOME

1

SUDDENLY, FROM THE DEPTHS OF AN OTHERWISE PEACE-
ful night, a name erupted from the past: Dolly Edwards, my
mother's friend, a smiling woman with very red lips and a fur
coat. I remember the coat because it was not removed for the
whole of her visit, which she no doubt intended to be fleeting,
having, she implied, much to do. There was another friend
from my mother's prehistory, before I existed, but this presence
was less distinct, perhaps not seen at such close quarters. Betty?
Betty Pollock? The Pollock seemed shifting, uncertain, an approximation. Maybe that had been her name before she married, for in my mother's day everyone got married. Women
wore their husbands much as they wore their pearl necklaces,
or indeed their fur coats. The shame that attached to unmar-
ried women was indelible, and my mother seemed to bear
something of that imprint although she was a respectable
widow. Dolly Edwards, with her flourishing presence, obviously felt sorry for my mother in her lonely state, with only an

eight-year-old child for company. Fortunately my mother did not perceive this, although I did. My mother was impressed by this visit, grateful, even happy. And Dolly Edwards played her part valiantly, reminiscing, producing names unknown to me and rejected by me as having no relevance to my own life. I may even have been jealous of this woman who had known my mother before her anomalous condition was confirmed by the death of my father. Truth to tell she did not much miss him: solitude seemed so much her natural state that Dolly Edwards was not mistaken in making of this a flying visit. My mother marvelled for days over this, with no resentment. It was less a visit than a visitation. It was never repeated.

The other friend, the one I thought of as Betty Pollock, though that might not have been her name, was less opulent, but kinder. This friend we actually journeyed to see, an event so rare that I remembered it. This visit occasioned no wistful comments from my mother, probably because Betty Pollock was not someone of whom she had learned to be slightly afraid. She was even rather unattractive, though clearly was not concerned by this, and in any event her large plain features were transformed by her dazzling smile. The other thing I noted about her was that she was happy. This was mysteriously apparent. I experienced it with relief, though I did not understand it. Now of course I can identify it as a state of steady satisfaction combined with an absence of longing. This must have been less the gift of her husband than of Betty Pollock herself, her smile signalling her contentment with her lot to all within her radius. She too had very red lips, though her hair was grey. She too was eager to reminisce, having nothing to hide. Yet my mother seemed inhibited in her presence, perhaps because of the contrast between them. I think that Betty Pollock vanished from the scene shortly after this visit: her husband was anxious to leave London and move back to Swanage, where he had grown up. I think my mother missed her, though not as much as she missed Dolly Edwards, who remained out of touch.

They had once been part of the same set, though this was a modest suburban affair, formed largely by parents who knew each other as neighbours or friends, and vigilant elder brothers who did duty as escorts when no other was available. I see Dolly as the bold one, Betty as the poor one, and my mother as the beauty, but whose beauty was undermined by an innocence that never left her. She longed for an ideal life which would not betray her, became married because her own mother wished it, and survived widowhood almost as a return to her natural state. I never knew a woman so inactive, her days reserved for reading and thinking. I soon learned not to disturb either process. Yet I think she was lonely, a perception that filled me with distress. We loved each other greatly, yet so exclusive was that love that it was experienced more like anguish. That feeling has remained with me and will no doubt survive all the rest.

It was therefore somehow appropriate that she should die and leave me bereft, and also appropriate, though unforeseen, that I should attach myself to a surrogate—though not a surrogate mother—whom I saw as capable of acting as a mentor. This was not a subject on which I was anxious to dwell, although it had no doubt accounted for my current wakefulness. That this wakefulness had produced only the completely irrelevant name of Dolly Edwards was one of those connections that the unconscious chose to make ahead of and perhaps more comprehensively than anything achieved by deliberate attention. Dolly Edwards was an associate, however negligent, of my mother. My mother was somehow not viable. It had become necessary for me to look for safety elsewhere, owing to my mother's frailty, her reclusive habits, and her early demise. At all times I had been fearful of leaving home in case something should happen to her. Yet leaving home had become a necessity, although a painful one, if ever I were to find freedom. The unconscious had a complete network installed: I had only to be patient and all would be revealed. I tried to work out the significance of what my abrupt awakening had tried to tell me. When the information came through it was not surprising: I had to undertake a journey. I had to leave home. If I had switched on the light I would have seen my travel bag, half filled, resting against my bedroom chair. What was marvellous about this was not the way in which the information had reached me but the fact that the entire process—waking, remembering, and finally coming to full consciousness—had taken no more than a few minutes, or even seconds. My impression of an endless night was erroneous, proof once again of the dark hinterland that produces our more useful understanding.

The circuitry was admirable. My eight-year-old self had seen that my mother had somehow been let down by her old friends. In Dolly Edwards's case this was easily explained: she was confident and affluent (the fur coat) and my mother was neither. Betty Pollock was a happy and satisfied woman, as even I had perceived: again, my mother was neither. In the days that succeeded these two encounters, disappointment had turned to sadness at her own inability to advance, and in the shadow of that sadness, only contained, only bearable if left undisturbed, I felt doomed to follow if I were not to make some sort of independent outbreak of my own, and on my own behalf. My best chance would lie in finding another source of authority, another agent of influence. I did not know whether this could be allowed, let alone arranged. It would be a journey away from home, symbolic no doubt but nonetheless real for all that. In any event it would have to be managed, and managed, if possible, without disloyalty, more or less invisibly, above all in good faith. I remain convinced that this is a critical task but not one which brings with it a resounding sense of victory.

In my own life very little has changed. I am older now, of course. I live alone, in a small flat, with the instinctive frugality of those who live alone, financially secure though never extravagant. I sit and write the book on which I have been working for some years now and which is almost finished, much to my publisher's surprise. In fact, despite the many delays, this tactic has served me rather well. The book is always immanent, but not in a position to be judged. The larval nature of the book pleases both one's friends and one's rivals. When questioned about its progress one responds with a certain smile, a smile that implies secret activity, and replies, quite truthfully, that one seems to have collected a great deal of material, so much so that the book may turn out to be more substantial than anticipated. I have seen this technique used to great effect by the worldly, so that the very absence of the book is more potent than its presence could ever be. In my case I can only plead an anxious sincerity: there *is* a great deal of material, and sometimes it seems that there will always be a reason for me to undertake one more journey, to revisit familiar sites and walk once again in deserted gardens, the only visitor on grey autumn mornings, until I realize that my work is truly finished. And that may be a very sad day.

My departures are all the same now, accomplished without difficulty but with a certain philosophical fatigue. Once I would have gone anywhere, strenuously; now I tend to go to the same places, which I know well, too well perhaps. I also see a few friends who have survived our now separate lives. Once we were familiars; now we are merely figures in the same landscape, and what had once been eagerness has become obligation. There is no blame attaching to this; the trajectory had been designed by the unconscious, a long time ago. But the unconscious does not rule the world, does not even illuminate it, apart from these brief fragments of understanding. It is, after all, only part of the self. The other part, the most important, is subject to the will. But it is also subject to the will of others.

2

I LEFT HOME ORIGINALLY TO STUDY IN FRANCE, THOUGH this was a decision I was happy to leave to others. I had expressed an interest in classical garden design at some point and this had been noted by my college tutors. Almost independently of my own volition I was provided with a scholarship from some benefactor's funds, and it was assumed that I should spend some time in France studying plans for ideal gardens, those which had been laid out in the seventeenth and eighteenth centuries and those which had existed mainly as ideals, sometimes offered as inducements to wealthy patrons such as Fouquet, some merely as emanations from the artist's mind. It was these last which fascinated me, the ideal archetype so perfect that its realization could only be an anticlimax. In fact it was the classical code—reticence, sobriety, order—that attracted me, and I thought it would be valuable to see these qualities laid out in observable form. Truth to tell it was the theory that shaped these gardens rather than the gardens themselves that was of interest: the creation of pure articulated space. Details of vegetation were irrelevant, as was the desire to impress. I was in search of a certain symmetry, a place of excellence that I should recognize and somehow make my own. I had no way of attaining this condition myself, but I felt that here was a concept that inspired a standard of behaviour far removed from the tame and unambitious customs that were my true inheritance. The design of the classical garden was an objective correlative, but a thoroughly acceptable one. It was out there, but it also corresponded to a disposition that I hoped to develop.

This exercise would also be valuable as a pretext for securing my liberty, more pressing now that I was no longer a child observing my mother's strange constraints, her inability to merge her experience with that of others, her silent days spent in mysterious rumination, but an adult of whom others seemed to approve.

Nevertheless, the act of leaving her to her fate seemed hazardous, though she accepted the prospect with equanimity. Garden design must have seemed to her completely irrelevant, as it occasionally did to me, but she saw that the wider world must be embraced at some point and that this was an appropriate way of severing the connection with our so quiet way of life and of making friends whom she had no possibility of welcoming, perhaps bearing in mind her own lack of success in this matter. My concerns, I thought, were less for myself than

for her safety, her comfort, when I was no longer there to en-
sure either. My own future seemed completely blank, but with
the prospect of those others who would take me in hand and
dictate my future for me. In order for that to happen I had to
be physically removed and if possible unwitnessed, for to make
such arrangements while still in my mother's orbit would seem
disloyal. Somewhere else such intentions could be given free
rein, without prejudice. Yet I was surprised at her calm acceptance. We should each be alone; that perhaps was a matter she
found so easy that she had no fears for me in my own coming
isolation. Nor did I. I was healthy and even confident; besides,
this leave-taking had been ordained for me by those others
who perhaps had my welfare at heart. There was a moment of
that so familiar anguish when we said goodbye (but with the
prospect of frequent visits home), and then I was gone.

There was no man in our family, apart from my mother's
older brother, a bachelor, who, I now see, supported us from
the income of my grandfather's investment in and ownership
of modest properties in outlying places we had never had the
occasion to visit. He bore this burden grimly, for which I disliked him. Had I had brothers I should have had a more realistic view of the world; as it was I relied on fantasy, knowing, or
at least trusting, that one day I should meet the ideal lover who
would complete my education. This task too would be left to
others. I liked the brothers of my friends and found it natural
that we should appreciate each other's company, and some-

times more, but I was in no hurry to accelerate the process which I found entirely natural. Yet the wistfulness that I felt as silence habitually settled on our quiet flat was identified, perhaps unconsciously, with the absence of a man who would have provided me with the information I knew I lacked. That was a man's function, as I saw it, and no amount of feminist propaganda could dislodge this conviction. My own father had died when I was three, and I had no memory of him; that is to say I was unsure of his worth. I felt that he had failed in his duty to take care of my mother, but at the same time I was determined that this duty should not descend on to me. My mother's brother would have been delighted for me to become my mother's support and provider—her husband, so to speak— and this was the real reason for my determination to leave home. Garden design was at the furthest possible remove from a sensible life plan; hence its appeal. Hence my acceptance of my fate, about which I felt curiosity rather than enthusiasm. At the back of my mind I knew that I could always return home. I also knew that such a return would symbolize a failure so profound that I might never recover from it. Nothing would be said, but that very silence, added to all the others, would be definitive.

Yet I had no notion of how I was to live in my new incarnation. My knowledge of Paris was hazy, confined to what was visible through the windows of the coach that took school parties on their way to exchange visits with a school in Cologne.

I imagined Paris as another version of the ideal garden, with parterres, fountains, straight lines leading to other straight lines, the whole thing precluding any unauthorized interruption. Though I knew that this was ridiculous I did not question my ability to master the ground plan. Some sort of habitation had been found for me in a student hostel, which I thought I might leave when new destinations revealed themselves. All this thinking was quite abstract, divorced from contingencies. I knew no one; my task, I thought, was to discover everything and thus to fill my days, and indeed my nights, with such sights and sounds as would form the basis of my new life. There was perhaps a slight unease, which related to my untested ability to function on my own. But then there would be others to guide me on my way. And I had no real fear, or if I had, that fear was incorporated into determination. I had to shed certain burdens which I had inherited from my mother, a tendency to melancholy, to rumination, an acceptance of solitude. I saw these characteristics as dangerous, as indeed they were, and I saw my mother as something of an anomaly in the world which I envisaged for myself and which I intended to inhabit, that world of straight lines leading to other straight lines in a design of perfect symmetry.

It was in this spirit of hardiness and self-consciousness that I said goodbye to my mother and my home, although when I saw her face at the window and her arm raised to wave to me— gestures more appropriate to a welcome than a leave-taking—

my spirit threatened to fail. I was grateful to the anonymity of the landscape, to those unknown and somehow savourless streets, and to the windows behind which people still slept, for it was Sunday morning. If I was aware of anything it was of silence, the peculiar Sunday silence which had always depressed me, and even disturbed me, for I thought it unnatural for life to be extinguished in this way, having no notion of the gratitude with which the week's work could be relinquished. The same silence enfolded my journey. Nobody spoke to me. At the same time nobody seemed to think that I was out of order. My feeling that I conveyed an air of competence emboldened me. When we landed in Paris I congratulated myself on having accomplished this rite of passage successfully. The rest, I thought, would follow.

My awakening was rude, as awakenings are supposed to be. The room I was assigned in the quasi-college complex was mean by any standards. It contained a narrow bed, a rudimentary desk and a chair, and I could see that no amount of embellishment would ever make it sympathetic. The corridor rang with shouts as my fellow inmates made their way to the communal shower-rooms, while I sat on the bed, my bag unpacked, wondering how I was to survive. From the small window the view was of a poor approximation of a park, dotted with unconvincing buildings designed to evoke an impression of home for the multinational crowd of Moroccan, Spanish, Dutch, Chinese students who were supposed to count themselves lucky to have found a lodging in a city which I knew instinctively to be too rich, too authoritarian, and too confident to accommodate unfledged creatures such as myself, and no doubt some others like me, for whom home had been abruptly displaced. I was moved—by hunger, nothing else—to follow a smell of coffee and found a canteen where I should have to eat every day, for there seemed to be nothing in that prospect other than those overlarge though gimcrack buildings that closed the horizon, no restaurants, no cinemas, nothing but gravel paths leading to other installations not unlike the one I was in. As soon as I could I escaped into the open air, but it seemed that there was nowhere to go, and I felt as if I were in a sort of prison in which natural boundaries were observed but not indulged. I spent the rest of the day wondering how soon I could leave. This was far from the emancipation I had promised myself, and it was with a feeling of despair, which has stayed with me to this day, that I realized that I had embarked on a course of action which was in fact too difficult for me. That feeling too has persisted, although to all intents and purposes I have lived a life much like any other. In those early days I was careful not to make friends, although my fellow exiles were friendly enough, in case I should be tempted to reveal my horrible unreadiness, only to encounter in return an expression of surprise, even of condemnation, from those who had managed the transition better than I ever could. That impression too has stayed with me.

Slowly, very slowly, I retrieved some sense of independence. I made my conscientious rounds of various libraries and print rooms, and discovered, somewhat to my surprise, that I found the silent atmospheres, the bent heads of the readers, reassuring. I also found a way to negotiate the physical and moral distance that separated my own poor lodgings from the glamorous and beautiful city to which I made my way every morning, and which I left, with sinking heart, every evening. I saw no way in which I could bridge that gap, knowing myself unequipped for decisive action. The docility of study, in which I felt at home, repaid me to some extent for the sheer discomfort of my life, and for a long time I was unable to decide whether this was genuine or merely a compensation I had worked out for myself. At any rate it persisted, so much so that I began to consider myself viable, albeit with that feeling of estrangement that was my initial experience of life away from home. The obvious solution was to find somewhere else to live, but I was constrained by my grant, which barely covered my needs. In a rare moment of resolve I decided to use up the money as expeditiously as possible and return to London, the work half-done but easy to complete at a time when I should have recovered some strength of purpose. I took to eating out on a Sunday, so as to mark the end of the working week, and found that a simple omelette at the Ruc, surrounded by vigorous talk and expansive gestures, did much to restore my appetite. I could see the way ahead, although I could not follow it. And on Sunday evenings, incarcerated once more, I felt that familiar lowering of the spirits which defined that home away from home which was now my lot. Mondays, which most people dislike, were my deliverance.

Gradually I came to know and love the city, not only for its most public attributes, its history, its monuments, but in small overlooked corners, unfashionable churches, outlying bus stops where I found a quieter, more modest population, suburban squares where children played. On my conscientious visits to what had once been real gardens, to Vaux-le-Vicomte or Marly-le-Roi, I came into more meaningful contact with my subject. In those dignified but deserted spaces I could appreciate the symmetry which I had once thought rigid. I now saw that it guarded a secret, and if it enshrined a certain melancholy it also celebrated a divine proportion. I became attached to their absent owners, sought out missing features. In the Musée des Arts Décoratifs I found designs for fountains, miniature obelisks, portraits of long-dead pug dogs, delirious landscape drawings of massive overhanging boughs and branches, as if the artist were trying to escape the constraints of that preordained symmetry. . . . I could sympathize with all of nature, and, by contrast, with the echoing spaces of the museum, not much visited, where only the occasional footstep, or the creak of the wooden floor, broke the silence. I realized that I was becoming acclimatized, that the disappointment and loneliness that I still felt could be dispelled by such encounters, and that although I was habitually unaccompanied I could summon up an agreeable remark, a fragment of conversation, so that at no time, or so I flatter myself, did I reveal the existence of the sobriety that had overtaken me in that most vibrant of cities and which has remained my most constant companion.

The formality which is the essence of the classical garden settled on me like a beneficent shroud, shielding my melancholy from intrusive eyes. But my work, my disguise, consoled me for what I was obliged to forgo: love, friendship, warmth, familiarity. It was only when I returned to that awful room that I was impelled to reflect on my lack of everything that makes a way of life desirable. Strangely I did not think too much of my mother, who was immutably fixed in my mind's eye, sitting in a corner of her sofa, with a book in her hands. I had no plans to return to her. My home-going instincts, which were strong, had widened, deepened, so that I thought once again of fabulous opportunities provided by others, leading me into a future that would encompass a real home, a home of my own. Though there was no sign of this, I kept it in the forefront of my mind and was thus enabled to confront the long empty days.

3

FRANÇOISE, MY ESSENTIAL POINT OF REFERENCE IN this strange enterprise—which I found benign but increasingly unrealistic—was not at her station behind the catalogues but was clearly audible in the stacks, undeterred by the anguished 'Mademoiselle!' from M. Bonfils, the librarian, who decreed a monastic quiet for the benefit of his readers. Françoise ignored this, and was, if anything, applauded for her flouting of correct procedure, was indeed greeted with a loving smile by the elderly scholars to whose desks she delivered the bulky volumes from which they derived those facts which would enable them to create bulky volumes of their own.

We had become co-conspirators, clearly but wordlessly allied in our unspoken desire to subvert the solemnity of the reading-room. On the surface she merely provided me with those pattern books and prints which I studied with the utmost application and docility, until the darkening sky beyond the tall windows signalled the end of the working day, but behind our apparent rectitude we were alike in experiencing a form of anarchy which was, if anything, directed towards those innocent bent heads which I knew were serious, admirable, dedicated, but which I was in no hurry to resemble.

Sometimes she dropped a note onto my open pages: this signified that we were to meet for coffee and a sandwich at midday in one of the cafés she favoured. My assent was equally wordless. In fact I was the only person to whom she did not speak. To others she expressed herself cheerfully and kindly, and in complete indifference to the rules. Even when M. Bonfils emerged from his office, not so much to reprimand her as to see what occasioned her ebullience, she did not much modify her loquacity. She appeared to know everything about everyone, enquired how the work was going, an enquiry that was always welcomed, even if the answer was delivered in muted tones. It was her departure to her desk, and the relative silence that followed, that signified the real start of the working day.

I had initially warmed to this universal friendliness—quite indiscriminate, quite unmotivated—and my first impressions were positive. She seemed to me a repository of goodwill of a sort I had not previously encountered. After the first few days of our acquaintance my eyes instinctively sought out her presence, and if she were engaged in one of her laughing colloquies with this professor or that I took pleasure in studying her mobile features and her splendid figure, which she did not seek to disguise with the sort of suitably drab garments that might have been thought suitable to her activities. Indeed it was part of her charm that she lavished her presence unstintingly on those so staid readers to whom she represented something between a daughter and a mistress. The only person indifferent to her charm was M. Bonfils, but he was also slightly frightened of her: her vitality, he seemed to know, might sweep him away, and so apart from his 'Mademoiselle!', which she largely ignored, he appeared to have made his peace with her potentially disruptive presence and to have declared a truce which was acceptable to both parties.

She was a striking woman, with bold Gallic features, not beautiful but more than that, electric with an energy that made her presence in the library dangerously welcome. Her face was alight with humour, as if she found her position quite ludicrous, but not so ludicrous as the owners of those bent scholarly heads. Yet she never showed any antagonism towards them, though she equally clearly thought them less than normal men, as if they were disqualified from the business of living, and for that reason to be treated as invalids. What she expected from a man was all too obvious, which made her kindness towards those incapacitated by the nature of their calling all the more remarkable. Before we had exchanged a few words I was fascinated by her provocative behaviour, and the way in which she tempered it so as not to alarm those to whom she presented not only the books they had requested but herself. I envied her for this. I also wondered, as no doubt did those others, how she maintained this good humour, and who was the lucky partner to whom she went home and who was no doubt responsible for keeping her in such fine condition.

Perhaps because of her appeal to men of all ages she did not much commend herself to women, which was where I came in. My studious calm appeared to please her; no doubt she saw me as harmless, and harmlessly receptive. Certainly she had observed my sobriety, and had decided that I was a suitable confidante, whose evident admiration she was not likely to overlook. Maybe she considered me initially as one of the un-qualified, the incapacitated, yet when we got to know each other she found me acceptable in other ways. I was her au-dience, but then I was also in some essential way the one to whom she could reveal herself without fear or favour. When she discovered that I was the daughter of a widowed mother, as she was, she found it easy to assume that we had a great deal in common, although this was in fact inaccurate. Surely, I thought, the mother who had raised so confident a daughter could hardly resemble my own, with her silences, her reclu-sion, her so discreet love for me. But Françoise appeared to consider her mother as much of a problem as I did mine. She did not, however, betray in any way the anguish I had long felt in connection with my mother; rather the opposite. Her mother, I gathered, was something of a cheerful antagonist whom she understood perfectly. Only the tie of possession, which they both felt, was stronger than this.

'You went home this weekend?' I asked, as we sat down in the corner we always sought out in whatever café she favoured at any particular time.

'Of course. I always go home at the weekend. My mother usually invites friends, neighbours, on a Saturday evening.'

'Relatives?'

'No, we have no close relatives, only distant ones. My mother and I are quite cut off.'

Her face momentarily clouded as she exposed their isolated condition. My own face must have mirrored hers; she gave the sort of rueful smile that was her version of candour. There was no need to explain; my useful function was to quiz her as if I were some sort of interrogator, well-disposed but objective, the sort of discreet official who simply desired to be in possession of the facts.

'And you drive back to Paris on a Sunday night?'

'Yes, and I'm glad to. That man is looking at you,' she went on in an uninflected voice. 'Don't turn round. He'll come over if he's really interested.'

'But I'm not,' I said. I was sincere: such approaches were for Françoise, not for me. 'Are you happy with this arrangement?'

'I'm happy to get back to my flat. Happy to get away from

my mother's supervision.' She laughed. '*Maman* thinks she can oversee everything. I am to marry the offspring of one of those so respectable neighbours, it doesn't matter which. Whereas I have other plans.'

'Why would you not want to marry?'

'I intend to decide what I want for myself. Oh, later on, perhaps.' She shrugged. 'But not to fall in with my mother's plans. She is the most conventional woman in France. I think she is frightened of what I might do without her there to restrain me. She speculates, of course. She thinks she has pandered to me by allowing me to live alone, at least part of the time. But I know she suspects me of having lovers, many lovers. Have you noticed how very correct women have unbridled imaginations?'

'Do they?'

'Well, what about you? You're correct enough. What do you think about?'

'Well, I think about marriage, oddly enough. If I married there'd be two of us to be a family. I'd like that.'

I did not tell her that I envied those young lovers who walked hand in hand, still less those elderly couples doing their shopping together on a Saturday morning. I saw their closeness as a bulwark against encroaching solitude, and I wanted it for myself. I did not see how random intimacies, of the sort Françoise favoured, could compare.

She laughed as she saw my expression. 'My mother would

agree with you. She thinks that anything less than marriage—
to someone she already knows—comes under the heading of
bad behaviour. You clearly understand that, even if you don't
like it. You know you can always borrow the flat at the weekend, when I'm not there. If you have anything on.' A passing
scepticism was present in this kind offer. She was clearly intrigued by my lack of attachments, though in an odd way she
was glad of it. There would be no occasion on which we would
be forced to confront each other. And she would show no
mercy if we were ever to be in competition. She knew this.
Even I knew it. Both of us accepted a possible antagonism
with equanimity. Both of us knew there is no chivalry among
women.

I had seen this flat of hers and had thought it murky
enough to justify her mother's worst suspicions. It was in the
Boulevard Diderot, in the twelfth arrondissement, and consisted of a bedsitting-room, a *cabinet de toilette,* and an awkward
annexe between the two containing a hot plate and an electric
kettle. The whole thing was dark, secretive; the only window
looked out on to a gloomy courtyard filled with the building's
accumulated dustbins. I could see no reason to cherish this
place, particularly as I knew that the house to which she returned at the weekends was rather grand, certainly large, possibly ancestral, and to judge from the photograph she had shown
me, a place of some consequence. She was evidently proud of
this house, even vain, but Françoise was not averse to display-

ing her advantages. It was all of a piece with her striking unembellished face, as if she were playing with a more advantageous hand than other women and had no need of special pleading. The flat was useful for obvious reasons, for obvious purposes. It was a place to which men could be invited, and, like Françoise, had no need of embellishment. I had no desire for such a flat of my own, although the house, to which she had issued a vague invitation, interested me more. I wondered at the contrast between the handsome house and the slightly squalid flat; the one seemed to contradict the other, but I supposed that the flat was all that she could afford. I have never been able to solve the mystery of other people's money.

What this flourishing of attributes made me feel was increased discontent with my own arrangements, which formed a subject of conversation in which she appeared to take an interest. She was intent on improving me, and I felt myself irresistibly drawn to this process, as if only under the direction of one more forceful and successful than myself could I take my place in the world. My room continued to impress me as truly dreadful; the only comfortable place to sit was on the bed, and even then it was preferable to lie down. This was in the prosperous late 1970s, and yet I lived like a pauper. I was too intent on staying within my means, for not to do so would mean asking my mother—or worse, my uncle—for money. And yet I was a little surprised that neither of them had offered, and deduced that we were so poor that we could not bear to discuss money, let alone ask for it. But I felt disbarred from normal pleasure, even the pleasure of returning home after a day's work. I had no arrangements of the kind envisaged by Françoise, and I supposed that this was fairly obvious, but I should have liked to entertain the possibility. Françoise was both intrigued and aghast at my solitary state and frequently enjoined me to break out.

'You'd be better off in an hotel,' she said. 'A room in a small hotel. It needn't cost too much. Can't you ask your mother? You can't go on living in that place at your age. Don't you want a man?'

'I'd like a man for company,' I replied. 'That's why marriage appeals to me.'

She surveyed me with a total lack of expression.

'My poor little Emma,' she said finally.

This was how this particular conversation usually ended. And yet, like water dripping onto stone, it finally had its effect. Would it be so terrible to explain to my mother that I was cold and uncomfortable in my present lodgings, and that I should have enjoyed hot baths like the rest of the civilized world? Contingent on this reflection was another, even more uncomfortable. I had not been home, had relied on weekly telephone calls from the post office to monitor my mother's well-being. Yet even this task seemed to be beyond me, as if entering that zone of silence in Battersea were tantamount to relinquishing my rights. Françoise's gift to me, apart from her unlooked-for friendship, was to encourage desires for expansion. She saw, as I did not, that I was in drastic need of a life of my own. So far this had not materialized, and she was indignant on my behalf, though only for a minute or two. She was too avid for her own satisfaction to waste time on so backward a pupil as myself. And yet she wished me well.

'I think I might go to London this weekend,' I said. I should be doing this at her behest, but also at my own. 'I'll see if we can work something out.'

'There's a small hotel in the rue Delambre, where a friend of mine stayed for a few months. And you can eat out. No more canteen food. Pouah!' Her nose wrinkled in genuine disgust.

And yet I knew that she lived on coffee and baguettes, was incapable of cooking a meal, relied on invitations to supply her with nutrients. And then, I supposed, there would be ample provision at the weekends. There was a cook, she had told me, one half of a couple, so that she need never worry that her mother was uncared for. That, I saw, was the cardinal difference between us: I would, however reluctantly, be drawn back by the fact of another's loneliness, though that loneliness frightened and repelled me. Even the thought of going home, even for a weekend, made me hesitate. I needed Françoise's determination, rather than my own, to put plans into motion. That was why her company was so good for me. That was why I did my assiduous best to meet her expectations, even though those expectations were so low that she derived a visible pleasure when contemplating the distance between us.

I thought it tactful to let this line of thought lie dormant. That too was part of my role, never to insist, merely to suggest, humbly, that I was grateful for her attention. It was always indicated that I respect the effort she was making on my behalf. I drank the last of my coffee and prepared to leave.

The man who had (perhaps) been looking at me glanced in our direction, picked up his briefcase, and made as if to move.

'I'll see you later,' said Françoise impassively.

It was my cue to get up. It occurred to me that she would not follow. I went out into the street. It was a matter of honour not to look back.

4

LONDON SEEMED SO ALIEN, SOMNOLESCENT IN THE HALF-light, as if the sun would never rise again. The contrast between the anonymous streets, the uncertain perspectives, and my rigorous ghostly gardens could not have been more pronounced. In the few months in which I had been away I had grown accustomed not only to a different landscape but to a different mind-set. Even in my reduced circumstances I was aware of sharper contrasts, bolder exchanges. I should now have to reacquaint myself with a more ruminative way of life. The people I saw through the window of the taxi seemed to walk with averted eyes, wholly possessed by some interior monologue, as if they had never exchanged intimate confidences and were now schooled in the kind of enquiries which made no reference to the emotions. I missed the boldness of greetings, offered to friends and strangers alike, that had been the commerce of my early mornings: even my daily journeys to the library had been enlivened by an emphatic salutation, as if I

were a legitimate inhabitant, going about an entirely honourable activity, just like those strangely confident people whom I
passed in the streets and to whom I offered an equally confident 'Bonjour!'

Here, I knew, I should have to accept a degree of indifference, as if I had not walked these streets all my life, should have
to modify eager curiosity—the sort of curiosity surely everyone must feel—into a dutiful consideration of the weather, of
the daily alteration in the light as the season changed from
winter into spring. There was indeed much to be noted in this
muted nature which cast its understated dominance over a
population schooled in acceptance rather than revolution. The
world was changing, had changed, yet I saw few signs of this
change in the comfortable half-empty approaches to my home.
Surely there should have been more ebullience, more movement? Only the traffic, moving with monotonous noisy insistence, seemed possessed of any purpose. And yet, when I got
out of the taxi and surveyed those so familiar landmarks, I saw
something amazing, a camellia bush in full bloom, as if this
were the compensation I should find here instead of the excitement, the purely urban excitement, to which I had become
accustomed. Nature, bizarrely, would propose advantages if one
would only lower one's expectations, if one could keep one's
eyes fixed on this universal endowment, as opposed to that
heartfelt intimacy which was one's most primitive need. Even
friends whom I should contact, and of whom I was in truth

very fond, would, I knew, regard me as something of a stranger, since I had not been present to intuit matters which they perhaps guarded from view, and which they preferred to keep to themselves, lest they reveal too much. . . . Circumspection, which I should have to respect, would keep all conversations within bounds. This should suit me, since I had no adventures to recount. Indeed I felt a certain shame that I was not able to impart news of lovers and thus show myself in a more interesting light. I could hardly expect my gardens to stand me in good stead. Yet I was eager for any sort of exchange, any sort of familiarity; part of me longed to be reabsorbed, anxious as I was to exchange those months of solitude and application for something warmer, more receptive, even kindlier, for that peculiar English kindliness which is built on indifference but which reveals itself in a half-smile, an uplifted hand, when two neighbours meet, and from which it is impossible to tell whether they are friends or enemies.

The flat—my home—seemed to be bathed in the same half-light as the surrounding neighbourhood: I remember how my mother would never take up her book until the daylight won the unequal struggle, how averse she was to harsh illumination. She stood at the open door to greet me, and I was filled with a rush of love as we embraced. She had her coat on: she was going shopping, she said, to get something nice for our lunch. I was to make myself some breakfast and keep all news until she returned. I thought this less than ceremonious; by the same token it was unsurprising, since we took each other for granted. We were each other's familiars, ghosts, even, and this was no occasion for full-blown expressions of feeling. The anxiety I habitually felt for the remnants of what had never been a family was also familiar. And yet I knew that what was left would have to do duty for what was missing.

'Rob said he would look in later,' said my mother, as if to confirm this. Rob was her brother, my uncle. I had never loved him, yet even he must be pressed into service in this simulacrum of a homecoming. 'He has news to tell you,' she went on. 'He is thinking of buying a house on the south coast. He'll keep the flat for when he comes up for a meeting. We shall see less of him, I dare say. However, I'll let him tell you all about it. Make yourself comfortable, darling. How long are you staying?'

I had planned to stay for a few days; now I saw my visit as something of an interruption. The great news was of my uncle's desire to move to a new house; the great event was not my presence but his impending absence. As brother and sister they were extraordinarily close; part of my dislike of him was rooted in my conviction that he bullied my mother into thinking as he did. My mother always extricated herself from his pronouncements, or discussions about finance, about investments, and returned to her book, leaving him with the impression that he had won the day. It was her only feminine stratagem, and I had never approved of it. Yet it had been successful in keeping the peace, and I now had to face the fact that I was about to send him into one of his habitual furies by requesting a modest sum for my own greater comfort. I summoned up Françoise's scorn, saw her expression harden as if she were there to witness my misgivings. I had not said how long I was staying. For a moment I felt something like nostalgia for my monastic but so far unquestioned way of life. I had not so far been accused of any crime. Now, I thought, I should be laying myself open to charges of selfishness. There was money to be discussed: no good could come of that, particularly as I had no idea of how much or how little we had to live on.

The flat, in a complex of uniform redbrick buildings, was as discreet as my mother's quiet temperament demanded. It represented everything in the way of comfort that I so singularly lacked. Large windows looked out on to railings guarding a strip of park. Equally silent were the living room with its lamps and sofas, and our bedrooms, separated from each other by a length of dark-blue carpeted corridor. I unpacked, filled the washing machine, took the first of as many scented baths as I could fit in, and tried in vain to relax. My mind was filled with fruitless calculations which I knew were unrealistic: this flat, or one like it, was what I wanted in Paris. With this flat, or one like it, as my setting, I could aspire to friendships of my choosing, parties, love affairs. This exuberance, which would be, and was, completely out of character, would be the transformation so tantalizingly out of reach. There was of course no possibility of my being able to achieve this, just as there was no possibility of radical alteration of my character, or an end to the hermetic self-absorption with which I had almost made my peace. I emerged dripping from the bath, wrapped a towel round myself, and made for my bedroom.

'Emma!' reproved my mother, who had returned so quietly that I had not heard her. 'What are you thinking of? Supposing Rob had seen you like that?'

My nakedness had shocked her, and her reaction to it had shocked me. But when I saw that my bed had been made up with fresh sheets and the covers turned down, my heart melted. This was the unspoken celebration of my return.

'What time is Rob coming?' I asked my mother as we ate roast chicken.

'I don't know, darling. He didn't say.'

He never did. His visits were random, like government inspections, intended to keep the workforce on its toes. The contrast between my mother and her brother had never ceased to puzzle me, the one so silent and passive, the other so strangely intemperate. It was possible that my mother was the one fixed point in an otherwise lonely life. A tall, almost handsome man, he had never married, though there had been many opportunities for him to do so. He took his obligations as ruler of the family endowment very seriously, too seriously, and yet the role suited him, as did my mother's reliance on him. He was immensely censorious, beginning each visit with a diatribe against the government of the day. He believed that he, and he alone, stood for traditional values, chief of which was an exaggerated form of family piety. It had often occurred to me to question this; latterly I had come to see it as a condemnation of undue fantasy or aspiration. Naturally my activities came under this heading, and his attitude to my work, or rather 'work', took the form of more or less tacit accusation. He thought me an unworthy addition to his arrangements, arrangements which took in my mother, her comfort and security, and not much else. She played her part in this and never challenged his assertions, content merely to absorb them. She knew of his objections to my absence, which must have been discussed on many occasions, though never with me. I believe it suited them both to have me out of the way, thus guaranteeing their original alliance, which must have been disrupted by her marriage and further by my birth. His dislike of me, as my father's child, was relatively undisguised, but never justified. I in my turn had learned to avoid him, which was not too easy as he tended to turn up unannounced. He considered our flat as an offshoot of his own domain, in no way separate or independent. For as long as I could remember he had decided to buy a house somewhere fairly remote, but nothing ever came of this. He was always threatening to leave, like a temperamental star who has to be cajoled back into line. The threat was paramount, and it was real, for I did not see how either of them would function on their own. But it made me uneasy to know that this would overshadow my own request, and that that request might be ignored in the greater interest of whether the two of them would survive apart, as they strangely did together.

'I expect he'll look in at teatime,' said my mother, clearing the table.

'Let me do that.'

I was already preparing to demonstrate filial concern, as I should be required to do as a token of good behaviour. At the same time I was determined to get away as cleanly as possible, taking with me the afterimage of bourgeois comfort that would remain the legacy of this visit, a comfort I was anxious to claim for myself. The negotiation, as I saw it, was simple, or could be if conducted by reasonable people. I needed a modest allowance, or preferably a lump sum, so that I could budget for the remainder of my stay. How long that stay might be I would not say; indeed I did not know myself. I thought my mother looked thinner, even slightly frail, and this disturbed me anew. I felt that I was obliged to worry on her behalf, and might be expected to continue to do so.

'Nice of you to grace us with your presence, Emma,' said Rob, sitting himself down and picking up the paper, as he usually did. 'I see that the prime minister continues to embarrass us.' There followed the usual criticisms, to which I submitted as to a ritual, like Christmas or Hallowe'en.

'Pour Rob a cup of tea, darling,' said my mother pacifically. 'And there are biscuits in the tin, if you wouldn't mind.'

He took this offering without thanks. 'The house fell through,' he said abruptly, as though we had been discussing this all along.

'Oh, I'm so sorry,' said my mother, who had heard this, or something like it, before.

'Money will soon be tight,' he went on. 'The way things are going.'

'I wanted to talk about money,' I broke in. 'I rather wanted to move to somewhere more comfortable.'

They both stared at me. Finally, 'Anyone would think you were planning to stay there,' said Rob. 'Are you mad? Your place is here, keeping an eye on your mother. You've had your adventure. It's time to get a job. Settle down. Here.'

'I have only a few weeks to finish what I'm doing. After that . . .' I did not finish this sentence.

'I could let her have something,' said my mother, addressing herself to Rob, not to me. 'I spend very little. It seems a shame not to let her do what she wants.'

'You know what you're doing,' shrugged Rob. 'On your own head be it. I must be off. Emma, come down to the car with me. There are some papers I want your mother to see. And it might be in your interest to familiarize yourself with business matters. Time you had your feet on the ground.'

He kissed my mother, patted her shoulder, and left. I trailed awkwardly behind him, and was soon standing even more awkwardly on the pavement, my head thrust through the car window as Rob fished in his briefcase. This pretext was soon abandoned.

'Your place is here, Emma,' he repeated. 'Your mother is not a strong woman. Inevitably she will need help. I need hardly remind you of your obligations.'

I assured him of my constancy, loyalty, and everything else, all the easier since I felt a flicker of guilt. At the same time I was determined to leave as soon as possible.

That night was uncomfortable. I lay wide awake in my soft bed, assailed by conflicting feelings. I hatched out a plan which I thought would suit everyone: my uncle would buy one of those houses which he periodically chose and just as periodically relinquished, and my mother would go and live with him, leaving me on my own to fulfil my destiny without interference. This, I could see, would be an ideal arrangement, symmetrical, orderly, like the plan of a classical garden. I would join them from time to time but physical distance would keep our relationship within decent, and again orderly, bounds. At the same time the archaic part of my nature longed to be reintegrated into a context in which I was known and had no need to explain myself. '*Un jour nous partons, le cœur plein de flamme,*' says the poet, and goes on to describe the bitter disillusionment we confront at the end of the journey. I was now rootless in two places, and those who had overseen my departure for France—those others in whom I placed my trust—had failed in their duty of support. I would, I knew, finish my dissertation.

And then? A humble job, in safety, in London, or a more hazardous life elsewhere? It hardly mattered which. The fact that
neither my mother nor my uncle had shown the slightest curiosity about my activities struck me as unnatural. I had failed
to take into account the degree of solipsism which identified
them both as siblings, and which, to a certain extent, excluded
me. That they were unaware of this was their saving grace.

At breakfast I explained to my mother that I must leave
on the following morning. She took the news calmly, but she
looked tired, as if she too had passed a bad night. Possibly she
had been entertaining the same thoughts as I had, with the same
mixture of emotions. We passed the slow day together, reading.
I was beginning to mirror her habits, her reclusion. When we
embraced it was wordlessly, as if we understood each other perfectly. Away from her it seemed as if there were no end to leaving home.

5

OBEDIENT TO FRANÇOISE'S INSTRUCTIONS I MOVED INTO
a small hotel, and at last began to think of myself as a citizen,
though any observer could have told from my excessive compliance, my anxiety not to infringe the rules, that I was nothing of the kind. My room was inexpensive and not very
comfortable, but at least I was spared the weak light, the rudimentary appointments, the ringing shouts in the corridor that
had pursued me as a student in that custom-made institution
which I now saw as superficially hospitable but in fact restricting. Gradually I adjusted to my new home, always on the understanding that it was provisional, that somewhere at the end
of this process I would accede to a real home, a home of my
own, rather more like the one I had left, and to which I had
no desire to return. I took to eating my meals in the café next
door, and in time developed a taste for more adventurous
food, conscious that I could form new habits, venture farther
afield. In this I was helped by the weather, which had become

lighter, warmer, and when I went out in the morning it was
with genuine pleasure that I noticed the increasing liveliness in
the air, the unmistakable signs of regeneration.

Also I had acquired a new companion, Michael, who had
the room next to mine and who, like me, was observing the
sort of respite that cautious people allow themselves before returning to the duties assigned to them by others.

'At last!' exclaimed Françoise, thinking her efforts well rewarded, her pastoral duties at an end.

She could not have been more wrong, and for that reason
it was as well that she knew little about him, apart from the cardinal fact that he was male. He was a shy, taciturn man, or
rather boy, a couple of years older than myself but even more
innocent, more wary. Half English, half French, he made some
sort of living teaching English conversation to French busi-
nessmen, whom he visited in the early evening at their homes.
He would then come loping silently back to the hotel, where
our paths crossed, I going out for my meal, he returning from
his. *'Pardon,'* he said in the doorway. *'De rien,'* I replied, and we
both essayed a hasty smile. From the copy of *The Times* I had
under my arm he deduced that I was English, and on that very
first evening he accompanied me, or rather followed me, to the
café. After that it was inevitable that we should become friends.

Like most friendless people he was awkward with friendship, yet I could not see that he was in any way disqualified
from closer ties. On that first evening he questioned me relent-

lessly, as if this were the way to establish a relationship. I did not object to this: it was a long time since I had been an object of such fierce scrutiny. In fact it was the first time. I could see that he was something of a misfit, and put this down to a faulty upbringing, which I was careful not to disturb. His poetic looks—the fine-boned face, the lock of hair which he did not attempt to smooth back—were largely misleading, for there was no romance in him. Having decided from my answers to his questions that I was no threat to his peace of mind, he accepted me as someone with whom he might spend a certain amount of time. I learned nothing about him that he was not anxious to divulge: he was as reticent as I was, and we met, not disagreeably, as distant members of the same family might meet, having acquired knowledge of each other's habits from the same source, though that source was left vague and undisturbed.

'Will you go home? Eventually, I mean?' This was the only direct question I ever put to him, for his life seemed to me as tentative as my own.

'Might hang on here for a bit,' was the reply, from which I deduced that money was no problem. Indeed he had the indifference to the future that only a moneyed background can provide, the attitude to discomfort that only the rich can display. He did a certain amount of writing in his room, and I assumed that he was an aspirant novelist or poet, although this he kept to himself. He explained to me, in a rare moment of confidence, never to be repeated, that if he told me what he was writing it would escape him, being too evanescent to be shared. I thought it better to respect this, which he took to be a mark in my favour. Nor did I tell him about my dwindling interest in gardens. We spent time together, ruminatively, without much conversation but with the assurance of automatic if unsought company. We went for long walks in the light evenings, and on the occasional Sunday we went to Malmaison or Saint-Cloud and sat in the gardens like a very old couple.

'And your *amoureux*?' queried Françoise.

I could not tell her that after an initial exchange our relationship was platonic, even celibate. I replied with a smile to her questions, knowing that they would soon cease. Françoise was not interested in anything that was not immediate. I had confirmed her original estimate of me, that I was timid, inhibited, backward, and altogether harmless. It was the last quality, which was authentic, that appealed to her, even if it made her attitude towards me one of curiosity. I was another species, one she had not formerly encountered; there was even a kind of wariness, which was expressed in a tolerant smile with which she covered her exasperation. For she was genuinely puzzled by my lack of boldness, as perhaps I was myself. It suited me to sit quietly on a Sunday afternoon, perhaps to eat an ice cream at a rickety iron table, as if I were still a child, by no means anxious to exchange this condition for a maturity that I sensed was not quite within my reach.

For myself, and perhaps for Michael as well, this was a

blessed interval. Neither of us had a clearly defined future; neither of us wanted to return to what we had left. All I knew of his background was that his parents lived in Oxford, where his father was a don: all I knew of his parents was that he called them by their Christian names, which I thought sophisticated. He knew even less about me. For what was there to tell? I regretted, not for the first time, my meagre family, and even felt slightly resentful that so little had been done to prepare me for life in the real world. True, my mother had disbursed the money on which I was currently living but the worldly instructions that I had perhaps expected had never materialized. I knew, hazily, that she wanted me to marry, to find someone who would be responsible for me so that she might regard her task as complete and spend the rest of her life peacefully reading. As for my uncle . . . There was genuine dislike there, and at this distance I could see that it was mutual. I preferred Michael and his blessed silences to the overt masculinity exuded by my uncle, who, I saw, had something of the same attitude as Françoise: from his point of view (and he was not wrong) I was unawakened, asexual: therefore I might just as well find an occupation for myself by attending to my mother, whom he saw as lacking in protection. I looked askance at their lack of concern for me, though this was precisely the attitude I appreciated in Michael. Perhaps I was aware of an absence of excitement, but considered this a sacrifice worth making. I had a genuine appreciation of his absentmindedness. When, after a few seconds of inattention, he would put a hand under my elbow as we walked up the stairs at the Métro station I felt privileged. Here was someone who did not think me in any way at fault. His belated courtesies were to me more enjoyable than the most extravagant of compliments.

From this I deduced that my inclinations were fraternal rather than romantic, that I preferred this kind of stasis to the rapid conquests practised by those women who had been liberated into behaving like men, and of whom Françoise was perhaps the ideal representative, although her instincts were so primal that she needed no indoctrination from outside agencies. And it has to be said that I had retrieved something in the way of caste from the presence of a man in my life. I loved him in the least restricted sense of the word: I valued him, respected him, respected his separateness. He in his turn was grateful for mine. Our gift to each other was simple companionship, wordless acceptance. We had delivered each other from a solitude that would eventually have saddened us. The memory of our brief physical closeness had left a trace, had reassured us, had persuaded us that we had no further need of it to make us friends. One daring Saturday afternoon we went shopping together but this was not a success. The red pullover I urged him to buy was politely rejected. My arm was seized and we left the conspiratorial atmosphere of the shop with something like relief. The experiment was not repeated.

Without his company I should have been not only lonely

but purposeless. I had almost enough garden material for my dissertation and could now think about putting it together. All I had to do was establish certain general points and work out connections between them. Fortunately no conclusion was required. The raw materials were there for my successors to attempt the same worthy analysis. I imagined pale students, like myself, confined to the same exiguous lodgings, and shuddered. My past seemed unenviable, but then so did my future. Perhaps for this reason I found it easy to live in the present. I devoted my best energies to this pursuit, and was determined to be happy. The returning sun invested my efforts with a protective aura. I recognized this interval for what it was, a pause between various duties. That, if anything, made it more precious.

Some of this attitude commended itself to Françoise, who ascribed it to sexual satisfaction. I took care not to enlighten her, and my reticence confirmed her suspicions. Instead I diverted her by taking an interest in her own affairs which she found equally commendable. I knew she took risks, but they appeared not to harm her. She was a hunter, who took pleasure where it was offered, never truly knowing her partners, affecting a gaiety which, although genuine, provided little in the way of intimacy. I persisted in thinking friendship the greater good; this too I kept to myself. There was no dishonesty in this, or none that I could see. When she asked me what Michael did I answered, 'He is writing a novel.' I somehow knew this to be true. She, in her turn, regarded me with a new respect. I had established my credentials, and at the same time invested my previously drab position with a certain lustre.

'Did you have a good weekend?' I would ask her, thinking back to my own.

She was too well-bred, too French, to pull a face, but a grimace was implicit in her answer.

'My weekends are all the same,' she said. 'They follow a pattern established by my mother when I was old enough to be paraded before her friends.'

'You never mention your father.'

'Dead, but not regretted. He was largely absent, and I suppose unfaithful. My mother never speaks of him unless she is referring to the house, which was of course his. She says I take after him. She dislikes that in me. She is determined that I marry advantageously, as she did. Never mind love: advantage is what counts in a marriage.'

'But I thought . . .'

'You thought I had escaped all that? To a certain extent I have. But every weekend I conform. She is brave, my mother; I owe her that. But she's relentless. An advantageous marriage for me will also supply her with the funds for the upkeep of the house. She loves the house.'

'As you do.'

'Yes.' There was a brief silence as we contemplated her destiny. 'You must come out with me one weekend,' she said.

'My mother wouldn't mind. In fact she might approve of you. You'd like the house.'

'Describe it to me.'

'Well, you've seen the photograph.'

I had indeed and had been impressed. The house was of fine stone, not quite a cube, a truncated part of what had once been something bigger, not quite a château, rather what would have been a manor house had the same style obtained in England. In the corner of the photograph I could see a ruin. 'The chapel,' she explained. 'Sacked in 1789.' Despite herself she was proud.

'Where is it?'

'Near Sucy-en-Brie. Completely isolated. One hears nothing.'

'A lost domain.'

She smiled. 'I see you've read your Alain-Fournier.'

'I understand your attachment to it.'

'It's the life inside it I'm not happy with. My mother has these strange friends. I say strange, although I'm used to them. But sometimes when I arrive from Paris I see how strange they are. A couple of elderly married people, and a widow with her son. This is all for the benefit of the son. And for me, of course.'

'Why are they strange?'

'They are all old. Older than my mother, who is not an old woman. Yet in their presence she acts like a dowager. She exaggerates. I think they see through it. They regard her as a bit of an actress, not quite up to their standard. And yet they turn up every weekend. It's become a tradition.' She shrugged. 'Well, there's not much to do in the country.'

'Where do you fit in?'

'Well, I play my part. In a way I accept that I have to, although I have different plans, as you can imagine.'

'Your private life?'

'My truly private life.'

'Will you do what your mother wants you to do?'

'Not if I can help it. It would be like becoming her. And she's a difficult, complicated woman. You'll see, when you come down.'

Her mother—Mme Desnoyers—did not sound complicated to me. On the contrary, she sounded all too monstrously simple, one of those classic matriarchs one reads about, or like the mothers of Roman emperors, determined to drive their sons, or in this case daughters, on to destinies they might not have envisaged for themselves. And with a will capable of outwitting the world. Why else did those hardened visitors turn up every Saturday evening? No doubt she was an equally hardened hostess, with worldly manners which they could not fault. They might, however, have perceived some flaw in her makeup, wondered about her ancestry, to which no reference was made. They may have felt the same way about Françoise: her boldness would have been apparent to those elderly visitors, as if their seniority gave them the insights they may have been denied in their earlier days. I was not anxious to meet such a mother. My own emancipation was all too precarious: I was living a makeshift life, not unlike that of Françoise in her dingy flat, determined to live her own makeshift life away from that controlling desire to force her to conform. I looked at my friend's handsome face, and saw, for the first time, an underlying sadness, as if she knew that age would take care of her destiny, even more than her mother could. Even she would succumb to seriousness, and realize that liberty has its limits, and that those limits become apparent however much one desires to ignore them.

Besides, apart from my genuine inability to fit into such a setting, of which I was well aware, I did not want to forgo my Sundays with Michael for the problematic crosscurrents of which I should be aware. Those Sundays would have seemed anodyne to an onlooker: an almost silent perambulation around a chosen site, in the company of other petit bourgeois couples out with their children on the one day of the week that they could call their own, with the treat of an ice cream a gesture made towards those same children who had perhaps been reluctant to accompany their parents and who were not mollified by such an inadequate reward for the boredom they had endured. Yet such pastimes suited me: I derived pleasure from the presence at my side of my so undemanding companion, aware that he too valued a presence as silent as my own. I was alive to Françoise and her friendship for me. But Michael was more than a friend; he was my brother. I knew that we should spend that evening, as we usually did, going round bookshops, reading a few pages in each, before walking home again through the festive night. So anxious was I for the sound of his knock on my door that I made signs of departure, leaving Françoise to finish her coffee alone. Her wry smile told me that she misread the reason for my haste. Impossible to explain to her that I was evading involvement and not running to meet it.

6

MY FIRST SIGHT OF FRANÇOISE'S HOUSE, L'ERMITAGE, constituted the first *coup de foudre* I had ever experienced. Others were to follow, but few could compare with that first sighting, when it emerged from thickly wooded country as on to an open stage, in a clearing which later proved to be extensive, part of the land it had once owned and to which it still had a claim. Sweetly situated on an east/west axis which prolonged the hours of daylight, its large windows were flooded with the sun of an advanced spring when I awoke on the morning after our late arrival the previous evening. Then I had registered only silence, absence, a dying fall of birdsong, perhaps the sound of a distant car, but once the door opened I became aware of black and white tiles, and then polished wood, and then above all the smell of an aromatic substance which I did not recognize. Françoise saw my expression and smiled. 'We make our own,' she said. 'It preserves the wood.' To the shadowy figure who had opened the door, *'Madame est de retour?'* At that moment Mme Desnoyers herself appeared from what I later knew to be the salon. *'Ah, te voilà,'* she said, and kissed her daughter briskly. Turning to me she held out a hand. 'Emma Roberts,' I offered. 'Fernand!' she called to the person who had opened the door. He picked up my bag and gestured me to follow him up a staircase at the end of a long corridor. All this had taken only a few minutes and was perfectly and wordlessly enacted. Such behaviour, such physical ease seemed to me to belong to a different sphere from what I had previously known. Here was space, lightness, beauty; more than any of these, here was authority. It was an authority that existed independently of its owners, and I understood instinctively how essential it was that such a house should be preserved, by the meanest calculation, if necessary, by a loveless marriage, by a financial understanding. I understood the full implications of Françoise's 'advantage' and endorsed them completely.

I was clearly expected to make myself scarce, since Françoise and her mother appeared to be having an argument downstairs in one of the rooms I had barely had time to examine as I followed Fernand to a small bedroom in which he placed my bag, indicated a cupboard containing a washbasin, and left. I had somehow failed to establish myself as a proper guest, of a kind to which the house was accustomed. I was keenly aware of this and wondered how I should fare with the owner of the house, whose very summary welcome I now had time to evaluate. Clearly I would fail to impress. I could only hope to be agreeable and inconspicuous, well-meaning and accommodating, useful in any way consigned to me. In fact I did not have a chance to be any of these things until the following day, when I was more closely examined by Mme Desnoyers in the brief moments of attention she could spare from activities which seemed to take her all over the house, her heels on the wooden floors heralding her appearances which were rapid and unexpected, but which seemed sufficient for her to inspect my appearance and perhaps to witness my dreamy look of admiration and the obedient smile which was apparently all she required by way of a greeting. 'Françoise will show you round,' she said, in excellent English. 'Then I suggest you go out. The woods are beautiful at this time of the year. And I hear you are interested in gardens. Françoise!' she snapped out, and again I was removed from any possible conversation by her original engagement with her daughter, which was sufficiently embattled to convince me that the utmost tact would be required in my dealings with this woman, together with politeness, deference, flattery, and admiration.

I thought this price worth paying in return for the beauty of the house. I was ready to play my part and almost sorry to follow Françoise out through high glass doors to a terrace overlooking a small ornamental lake. We spent the day in the open air, roaming the woods we had traversed the previous evening, not saying much. In fact there was no need to say anything: the rules of the game were apparent, and any remarks of mine would be ill-judged, or rather, superfluous.

We were allowed back for lunch, during which time I was able to examine Mme Desnoyers for myself. A small, powerfully built woman, who had recourse to a bottle of pills by her plate, she appeared both formidable and frail; a frequent asthmatic intake of breath punctuated her questions to me, again in English, which placed me as a guest not destined to be an intimate, since these alternated with her remarks to Fernand, who brought in dishes of indifferent food, and Françoise, who replied with unaccustomed meekness. My references to my mother were well received; they placed me as a daughter who was in all respects cast in a mould of recognizable subservience, though this was not what I felt. I tended, almost in spite of myself, to supply her with what she wanted, a distant image culled from who knew what stereotypes, and which she seemed to prefer to the all too palpable presence of her own daughter, whose expression, though neutral, indicated a tendency to disagree which I knew from my own conversations with her. Indeed I knew about the situation from these conversations, and was confirmed in what I had learned by the silent opposition of two strong wills, anxious, on this occasion at least, to let none of this opposition break cover. At the same time the similarity between them was unmistakable. They had the same almost Roman features—the straight brows, the firm lips, the powerful nose—that in Françoise combined to form extreme handsomeness and in her mother an expression of pure will.

Mme Desnoyers was dressed in a pair of black trousers, as was Françoise, and a black jacket which had seen some wear. A silk scarf was draped negligently round her neck, and her still black hair was swept back sternly from her forehead. 'Your mother lives alone?' she enquired, and when, ploughing on through an evident lack of interest, I went on to describe our modest flat, and my mother's equally modest habits, she relaxed slightly. Obviously I was supplying her with the information she wanted: it was established that my mother owned her own home, had no need to earn her living, and was supported by family money. This placed her in a favourable category as a woman of some independence, an enviable state which had the virtue of supplying me with a modest though respectable rank which might otherwise have struck her as puzzling: I lived in an hotel, sat in a library all day, and was not in the business of making myself attractive to men. All of this was commendable: I was a good daughter. She even favoured me with a more considered examination, perhaps comparing my looks with those of her more striking offspring. My cheeks burned as I realized that I was not adequately prepared for this degree of formality. I had brought no change of clothes with me, thinking my grey trouser suit presentable if not smart. I was informed that after dinner that evening she would be receiving certain guests who were in fact old friends, and that she was sure they would be

very interested to hear about my work on garden design. There
followed another asthmatic intake of breath. *'Maman!'* warned
Françoise. Mme Desnoyers placed a hand on her breast, and
said, 'Until dinner, then.' When she got up to leave we both
stood respectfully until she had left the room.

The contrast with my own mother could not have been
plainer. My mother, a pretty though faded woman, whose active life was all too clearly behind her, made little physical im-
pact, dressed simply in skirts and cardigans, and though no
doubt satisfied with my appearance made no attempt to im-
prove it. I did not possess the sort of clothes that were called
upon to make an impression, nor was there any need for them
to do so: we knew few people likely to visit, kept no servants,
and went to bed early. Even I, in the hotel, went to bed early. I
was too introspective to enjoy unfamiliar company, which was
why I so appreciated the company of the equally undemonstrative Michael. It was only with Françoise that I discussed
weighty matters of will and desire, and even with Françoise I
did little more than listen. I thought, with a certain discomfort,
that perhaps my mother should have done more for me in the
way of instruction, of preparation. I was almost angry with her
until I reflected that such anger as I felt should more properly
have been directed against myself. Mme Desnoyers was of a
different order. Her daughter, as I knew from that daughter,
was a counter in the great game of possession and advantage;
she was to obey, and only then would she be obeyed. She was

to secure certain benefits for her mother—status, her continuance in the house, indeed the house itself—by a judicious bargaining of favours. Mme Desnoyers had no doubt that this could be managed. The looks she gave Françoise were full of laconic pride, as if she could well imagine the steps that would have to be taken, the stratagems needed to bring about the desired result. She evidently shared the same disposition she was determined to repress on her daughter's behalf. And Françoise knew this. She in her turn recognized her mother as a model, and in her reluctant, even rebellious way, felt an equal pride.

My sartorial misgivings were confirmed later that same day. As I had feared, both Françoise and her mother had changed for dinner. Dinner itself was served by Fernand in a slightly grubby white jacket, as if he too were bound to observe certain rules, or rather, forms. I sat with my trousered knees all too prominent, rising to my feet as Mme Desnoyers and Françoise appeared in silk jackets and flowered skirts. They had a sudden look of beauty. If anything Mme Desnoyers outshone her daughter. She had, I saw, a fine figure, although she carried too much weight, and her face had been more clearly defined by the judicious application of colour. She looked to be almost a contestant on her own account, whereas Françoise, in comparison, was almost subdued. Clearly these clothes were kept in reserve for purposes of conquest, and I wondered at Françoise's decision to lower her sights to her habitual makeshift lovers when she could so easily have followed her mother's example and played for high stakes. But then I reflected that Françoise entertained desires of her own, and was not willing to subordinate those desires to the ruling of another. 'How lovely you look,' I complimented Mme Desnoyers, wondering if this compliment were a little too familiar to be appreciated. But it was received with a gratified smile which reassured me. She seemed to be in excellent humour, which was just as well: her gaze contained complicity as well as decree, a decree that this game was to be played according to the rules, her rules to be sure, but ones with which Françoise would eventually comply.

The guests arrived at nine, at an hour when, soporific after a day spent largely in the open air, and slightly dazed from the effort of giving an account of myself, I was almost ready for bed. They consisted of four couples: Dr and Mme Bachelard, Monsieur and Mme Dulong, Mme Brunet and her ancient mother, and Mme de Lairac and her son Jean-Charles. In fact it was only the latter two who were significant. Mme de Lairac would in fact have been significant in any company, a woman with the assurance of inherited wealth and the slight air of disdain that accompanied it. Her son, Jean-Charles, was a pale, slightly corpulent man of indeterminate age: his flicker of interest when we were introduced was immediately dowsed when his mother laid a hand on his wrist. The rules of the game were apparent. Jean-Charles was the prize, Françoise the sacrifice. Mme de Lairac wanted the house, Mme Desnoyers wanted the money. It occurred to me that she and Françoise were poor, a fact reinforced by Mme Desnoyers's excessive amiability. Gone was the air of distraction, the implication of hauteur; now she was all enthusiasm, almost excess, a fact noted and enjoyed by her adversary, Mme de Lairac—Madeleine—who contributed little to the conversation but enjoyed the advantage of genuine superiority. This had the unfortunate result of casting some doubt on Mme Desnoyers's background, which was never disclosed, not even hinted at, her change of demeanour into actressy warmth, with many references to *'mon pauvre mari'*, which were not quite what was expected in this setting. A glass of wine was served: the wine was markedly superior to the food we had eaten at lunch and dinner. Since I was there to contribute little more than background noises I said my piece on gardens, and added how fortunate I had been to meet Françoise in the library where I conducted my research. This was well received, and Mme Desnoyers—Marie-France—appeared relieved that her daughter's function and status were recognized. After that I contributed even further by devoting myself to the old lady, Mme de Freyssinet, who rewarded me with a smile of great sweetness, but who was, I subsequently discovered, almost completely deaf. In any case I was disbarred from the general conversation, which was of local affairs, local politics, and mutual friends and neighbours. Just as I was wondering how much longer I could stay awake, Dr Bachelard signalled the order of release by referring to his wife's delicate health, with which they were all familiar, and decreeing that she must not get overtired. Leave was taken. The entire visit had lasted a bare hour and a half.

In my room I thought of Jean-Charles and his adamantine mother, both to my mind unbearable, the son even more than the mother, though he had said and done nothing that was less than polite, even courtly. It was his appearance that offended me. A pale and costive-looking young man—but how young or rather old was he? Thirty? Forty?—he had the look of one who had come up through the best schools and risen to that most esteemed of French professions, civil servant. In fact he worked in a bank, as I had learned from Mme de Lairac's throw-away remarks, as if she were advertising his worth. She had to do this, as he was virtually silent. He was tightly buttoned into the sort of blazer I had seen in the windows of Old England and which did little to disguise an incipient paunch. Certainly his attitude to his mother was exemplary: he hovered over her like a waiter in an expensive restaurant, but I felt indignant on Françoise's behalf. Such devoted sons rarely appeal to the women they marry, or are instructed to marry. Françoise her-self looked particularly handsome that evening, although her unaccustomed flush may have been prompted by annoyance. Something more heroic might just have won her over; in fact a show of rebellion, or just polite boredom on his part, might have served to incline her in his favour. Even a mother might have appreciated some sign of independence, but Mme de Lai-rac merely cast an eye from time to time over the handsome appointments of the salon and did not protest against its chill. I noted that she had provided herself with a silk shawl which she drew protectively round her shoulders as the evening progressed. To each of her minimal utterances Mme Desnoyers responded with enthusiasm, but she did not attempt to detain her guests, all of whom knew the form the evening had taken. As Françoise had said, there was not much to do in the country. I had no doubt that the ritual would be repeated in the days, weeks, months to come. For that reason alone it would be desirable to break the monotony, but it would take something equally ceremonious in order to do so. Either that, or some act of violence, which would be unthinkable.

I slept badly, in my hermetically sealed bedroom. The following morning Fernand failed to appear with my coffee, all that was apparently required in the way of breakfast: bodily needs were not much catered for in that household. But the house itself looked even more beautiful in the early morning, as I made my way out onto the terrace and walked round to the main entrance. This was how I should think of it when I was back in Paris, pristine, impervious to human intentions, and even to human inhabitants, whoever they turned out to be. I should like to have left at that point, but I was reliant on Françoise and her car. I was sure that Mme Desnoyers would have wished me to have left, certainly to disappear before lunch, if lunch there was to be. The servants were surely absent on this Sunday morning, and although intrigued I was rather hungry.

It seemed polite to linger downstairs until someone—Françoise or her mother—appeared and to take my leave, with fulsome thanks that would be entirely genuine. I wondered if by any lucky chance there might be time to catch Michael before he left the hotel and started out on a walk. I wanted to discuss this almost theatrical weekend with someone, though I was aware that he would be largely unresponsive.

When Françoise appeared she was carrying my bag, which I had already packed. 'We can go as soon as you like,' she said. 'My mother says to say goodbye to you. She has enjoyed your visit and hopes you will come again.' I doubted whether she had said any of this, but I expressed equal gratification and sent the appropriate messages to my absent hostess.

'*Maman* is not too well this morning,' said Françoise, her face clouding over. 'Her breathing is bad. These evenings are quite a strain on her. And the upkeep of the house . . .' Her voice trailed away. 'And Fernand and Mariette are getting old and are threatening to retire. They won't do so, of course, but if they did . . .'

'There are agencies,' I pointed out.

'Pouah! Foreigners. My mother would not consider them suitable. Are you ready?'

She was so anxious to leave herself that I was almost bundled into the car. We drove in silence through the beautiful morning. There seemed to be no other cars on the road, and few houses. I was removed from the house's sphere of influence, and was half regretful, half relieved. Françoise evidently felt the same.

'I'm sorry it was so boring,' she apologized. 'You were very good.'

'I loved it,' I said truthfully.

'You see what I'm up against,' she said, but her heart was not in it. She was bound by a complicated loyalty which could only be shaken off as the physical distance between herself and her mother increased. '*À demain,*' she offered through the window of the car, as she handed out my bag. Evidently there was to be no further meeting that day. I, on the contrary, longed to place the whole incident on record. Back in the hotel, which now looked shabby, I knocked on Michael's door, but there was no reply. I stared out of the window at the familiar street and wondered what to do with the rest of my day.

7

THAT NIGHT I HAD A DREAM OF BLISS SO RARE THAT I knew it was unconnected to anything I had ever experienced. The details immediately escaped me when I woke, but I knew, simply and conclusively, that I was loved. I was left with an impression of golden light, but this light had nothing supernatural about it, almost the opposite; it was the light of the sun in midheaven. What this dream signified was unclear, as were the circumstances that had brought it into being. Maybe the mere fact of eating at someone else's table was responsible for the feeling of being included, or maybe it was a warning that the circumstances of my present untethered life were inadequate. I also knew that Michael could not supply this intimation of completeness, and my disappointment that he had not waited for me was dispelled by the knowledge that he was not and could never be the agent of my happiness. In the light of this dream I dismissed my customary timid pleasures and realized that something else was called for. Yet there was no sign of this, or what it was to be. It simply put into place the mild diversions of the weekend, which I now saw were emanations, echoes of other lives, and not of my own.

At other times, and perhaps until then, I had been amenable, passive. I considered myself, in outward appearance at least, virtually French, walked the streets with vigour, drank my coffee black. The possession of a little money had given me assurance, yet that money was limited, and I should soon have to go home. I also knew, in the light of that dream, that my work was not only cursory but humdrum, that any further work I did would not supply the illumination I had glimpsed. I even wondered if I might abandon the work already completed, let it slip into that limbo in which all unpublished theses reside, with the promise to my superiors that I would continue my researches and that they would eventually come to fruition. Maybe this was true, yet the prospect was unattractive. Unfortunately there was nothing else within my grasp, nor, it seemed, could I hope to conjure an alternative into being. The gift of such happiness, the happiness of the dream, although entirely human—for I knew it did not pertain to the hereafter—was arbitrary. One might or might not encounter it, but only as a gift. So unmistakable had it been that I knew I should remember it, whether or not it was ever to be repeated. It seemed that even this was unlikely. Beautiful as the feeling had been, its only effect was to expose a condition of longing, and the knowledge that it must be sought, but also that it might not be found.

I wondered what to do with this new day, which promised to be fine, too fine to confine me to the library. In any event Françoise had intimated that she did not expect us to meet, and I thought it better to let a day or two elapse before we resumed our normal routine. Michael, I knew, would be invisible: it had somehow been decreed that we should not meet in the daytime, but only in the evenings and at weekends. This ruling was unformulated, but neither of us thought to question it. The mere fact that I went, as it were, to work every morning, leaving him in situ all day, had so far suited us both, but now I saw that it constrained me to keep on doing the same thing every day, when in fact I had less incentive to tinker with footnotes in an attempt to convince myself that this was a useful activity. To do so on this particular day, and even more so on the days that followed, would be mere pretence. This frightened me: instead of leisure, freedom, this suspension of routine had a feeling of remission, as if by abandoning my harmless task (and it was after all quite respectable) I was laying myself open to all sorts of extravagance, depredation, and a kind of inventiveness which was not in fact in my nature. There were no witnesses: no one would deplore my absence, or indeed question it, yet the prospect of an empty day was not reassuring. Moreover it did little to mask the greater problem of how to continue, now that this licensed interval was drawing to a close, may even have ended quite definitively before I was properly aware of the fact. This would mean that I had no further reason to stay in Paris, yet my life in the library, the hotel, the café, had suited me until I became aware that it was in all respects inadequate. That had been the import of the dream: beauty had been revealed, either real or imagined, and I could no longer live with its absence.

I wrote a note of thanks to Mme Desnoyers and went out to post it; beyond that I had no plans. The day was radiant, though an acid wind was there to remind one that it was still April, and that the light was not yet that of the settled days to come. Nevertheless there was an almost palpable air of renewed enthusiasm in the steps of passersby, in greetings to neighbours, to café owners, to waiters who appeared on the doorsteps of restaurants to sniff the air and to extend the city's hospitality to their regular patrons. It was impossible to contemplate leaving all this for London, which I perceived in apocalyptic terms, grey, lowering, morose, whereas in fact it was a comfortable city in which to live, and in comparison with my present arrangements positively luxurious. Yet it lacked the essential component of flair, which even one as undemanding as myself could appreciate, in the mere sight not only of the grander streets but of one's own humble surroundings, one's own Métro station, bus stop, stretch of pavement. Thus its glamour was available to the merest and most temporary inhabitant and would remain in the mind of such a transient as an image of the ideal city, a reputation it strove strenuously to uphold.

Knowing the day to be a lost cause, I set out to walk to

the Luxembourg, thinking I might cast a critical eye on the
layout of the gardens, though I had no need to do so. Instead I
might just sit there and try to work out a plan for the future,
for I should have to get a job, forswear days such as these. Indeed the feeling that my liberty was already compromised, that
the day of my departure was imminent, lessened the pleasure I
might have had from sitting on an iron chair and watching the
children playing, as I was fully entitled to do, to squander time
that had suddenly become precious, as if time were entirely irrelevant. I may have thought this almost questionable inactivity
might predispose me to another session with my footnotes, to
an almost welcome return to my previous confinement. In the
meantime I determined to explore this unearned leisure which
was, after all, under threat from obligations of various kinds.
Yet that now vanishing memory of beauty, revived by the almost cloudless sky, the children playing, determined me to stay
in this place, if possible forever, to find work of some sort, to
trust the temporary nature of such a way of life as being more
realistic, indeed more sensible than the settled comfort to which
I had once aspired.

I ate a sandwich for lunch, walked to the Louvre, lingered
in the company of Roman statues, and finally, with a sigh,
made my way home, for this was how I might now think of
it. My room seemed to me almost intolerably cramped, but I
made my peace with it, for this was how I now should have to
live. Even the light through the window seemed meagre, re-

calling me to order. The knock on my door startled me, as did Michael's appearance; he rarely entered my room unless invited to do so, but now his expression was wary, his eyes evading my own. I was disposed to welcome him but he ignored my remarks and handed me a slip of paper.

'There was a call for you,' he said. 'From London. A message. I thought it would be better coming from me. I've read it, I'm afraid.'

I unfolded the paper and gazed at the familiar telephone number. I was unwilling to read the message, which could only be bad news. I knew what it signified, and was entirely correct. My mother had met with an accident. No details were given. I handed the paper to Michael, too faint suddenly to speak.

'I'll stay here while you telephone,' he said, and it was the kindest thing that anyone could have done, for when I asked for the number my uncle, Rob, answered and told me that my mother had died suddenly while out shopping: an aortic aneurysm, he said, his voice choked with tears. Death would have been instantaneous. Then I did faint. Michael must have taken the telephone from me and heard the news for himself.

When I recovered he said, 'You'll have to go home. Are you fit enough?'

'Yes, I must go home.'

'I'll take you to the airport. Do you want me to come with you?'

'No, I must do this alone.'

He nodded. 'If we leave now you can be in London by midnight. There's no need to pack, or anything. Although I suppose you'll need to stay for a bit. Until . . .' Until the funeral, he meant. 'Ring me at any time,' he said. 'You'll keep the room, I take it?' It was my turn to nod. 'Let me know when you're coming back.' He took my hand and held it. Then he picked up my jacket and held it out to me. I handed him my shoulder bag. He examined the contents. 'Yes, you've got enough for a single ticket. You can book the return at the other end.' For there would surely be a return, he seemed to be saying. And then it was time to leave.

I knew nothing of the journey. I may have slept, or perhaps lost consciousness again: it hardly mattered. But ever since then sleep or the approaches of sleep have been accompanied by a feeling of terror, of omens. It was not until the plane landed and I was out in the cold night air that I was aware of being alone and wished that Michael had come with me. But this was a task I had to perform alone and would have to continue to carry out until such time as I should be allowed to forget it, or if not forget—for who could forget this?—to consign it to a past I was not eager to relive. All I could hope for was oblivion, or some form of amnesia, yet I knew that I should have to stay awake, remain vigilant, although a perverse drowsiness slowed my steps as I made my way out into a solitude greater than I had ever known. 'Careful, Miss,' said a voice, and almost absentmindedly I stepped out of the way of a baggage cart. There were few people travelling. They would all have looked the same to me even if I had known them. I found a taxi, a piece of luck at that time of night, and reached the flat in the early hours. I sat down in a chair, careful, even in that extremity, to avoid my mother's place on the sofa, and foundered again.

I was awoken some hours later by the sound of a key in the front door, and stood up, dazed, to meet my uncle. He looked shabby, red-faced, as I had never seen him before, and if this could happen to a man like Rob, who would be there to sustain me? He began to cry, which terrified me; I had never seen a man in tears before. I smoothed my hair, anxious to impart some normality to the scene, and wondered whether he intended to move into the flat. This would have to be established straightaway; there was no possibility of our cohabiting, and I should, without a qualm or a moment's hesitation, leave him there, renouncing all rights, careless of the future, if he would only leave me alone. His grief seemed excessive to me, noisy; my own eyes were dry. Only the hammering of my heart and the tremors in my hands told me that this shock was like no other, and must be endured.

'What happened?' I managed to ask.

This brought on a fresh bout of weeping. 'She was out shopping. In Selfridges, as it happens. She simply collapsed and died. Immediately. That's what the medics told me. Death was instantaneous. They found my address in her bag. There was a card there with my number on it. "In the event of my death," it said, "contact Robert Moore." It was signed with her name, and gave her address.'

'Where is she now?'

'At the undertakers. I saw to all that.'

'Thank you.'

'Of course you should have been there. If you'd stayed at home, as you should have done, none of this would have happened.'

'But there was no warning. How could it have been prevented?'

'You knew how frail she was. And you hadn't seen her recently. You didn't have the decency to come home regularly to check on her. . . .'

This was true. I had had in reserve the knowledge that I should eventually have to come home for good as my excuse, and my weekly telephone calls had provided some form of reassurance that nothing in her situation had changed. Or perhaps, I thought, I had decided this for my own benefit.

'The least you could have done was keep her company,' he went on. 'It was all left to me, as everything always is, always has been. Your father was useless, and anyway I was against the marriage. It's not as if we were a large family. You were her next of kin. And she was lonely.'

Yes, I could see that she was lonely. That was what was unforgivable. No one should live as my mother had done, perhaps keeping to herself intimations of a weakness that was not of the mind but of the body. I knew nothing of this, and I suspected that she had not confided in Rob, whose ever-present indignation would perhaps have rebounded on her, making her life even more wearisome. She had spared us both, only to shock us at the end.

'I shall never forgive you for this,' he said, stowing away his handkerchief. 'And now I must arrange for the cremation. You'll have the grace to attend, I hope? Not too many social engagements in Paris?'

This spurt of anger seemed to enliven him. 'I'll have a cup of tea if you can spare the time.' The look on my face must have sobered him. 'You should eat something, I suppose. Well, you'll have to look after yourself now.'

It was at that point that I knew that I should never willingly set eyes on him again. He knew it too. Only my mother could have reconciled us, and she was no longer there. My only reflection was that he would have to go without his tea, and for a while I felt badly about that.

I wandered into my mother's bedroom, saw her neatly made bed, opened the doors of her wardrobe, and found everything in order. Already these things looked like relics. Rob, or the police, had brought back her bag, in which there was a lace-edged handkerchief of which she was fond. This I took for myself. In the kitchen her cup and saucer stood on the table, awaiting her return. I did not see how I could ever live in this place, and yet I knew I should have to. I stood by the window of the sitting room and looked out, as if to see her coming home. Yes, she was lonely; I saw that all too clearly. Her life was not the sort of life lived by a normal woman. She was on good terms with everyone—neighbours, shopkeepers, the caretaker—yet intimate with none of them. I should have thought her days entirely empty had I not had some knowledge of how to spend such days on my own account. This training in solitary pursuits was what united us both, and I began to think of her not as someone utterly lost but as a stoical veteran, more resourceful, perhaps, than many of her contemporaries, none of whom seemed anxious to seek her out. They would think such stoicism unseemly, unnecessary in an age of instant communication, of almost obligatory female solidarity, of intemperate confidences. This was not her way, nor mine, but it seemed as if we bore the same marks. I should have to refine my technique if I were to match her courage. Either that or turn my back on such a legacy completely and make my way into an indistinct future.

At some point the caretaker, Mr Morris, came up, having met Rob on his way out and heard the news. He seemed sincerely affected, was disposed to stay and reminisce, not only on my account but on his. 'Such a kind lady,' he said. 'Always asked how my boy was getting on. Always well turned out. I like to see a woman take care of herself. You'll be staying, I take it? If not, let me know. I'm always getting enquiries about these flats. If you think of leaving . . .'

'I've not had time to think of that,' I said. 'But of course I'll let you know if I decide to make any changes.'

'Anything I can do,' he assured me.

After that the doorbell rang several times. Kind neighbours, avid for details, came and went. One old lady, whom I barely knew, presented me with a dish of stuffed peppers. This moved me unbearably, though I doubted whether I should ever be able to eat again. As it was getting dark Rob let himself in again, dumped a bottle of milk on the kitchen counter, and said, 'Friday, Golders Green. Eleven a.m. You can get there by yourself, I take it? Or do you want me to pick you up?' His dislike of me was undisguised.

'Oh, no,' I said. 'I'll get a cab.'

I was surrounded by the amenities of a comfortable, even prosperous flat, and yet I abjured them all. Though I was hot and exhausted I would not take a bath, lay claim to my bedroom. I even unplugged the telephone, though not without a thought that I should ring Michael and tell him that I should be away, for what? A week, perhaps. On reflection it seemed more appropriate to write him a letter, for I did not trust my voice. This I could do on the following day. My mother was strangely absent. This anomaly I accepted as I finally realized that she was gone. Then I went to bed, and waited, terrified, for sleep.

But sleep did not come. Perhaps it was the prospect of the days ahead that kept me awake. I stared into the dark and unfamiliar night, with strange cars passing in the street below, and wished for it all to be over, whatever it was to be. It seemed impossible to remember that less than twenty-four hours earlier I had loitered in the sun, thinking myself entitled to an interval of leisure, sitting at a café table, looking forward to seeing Michael, even looking forward to a resumption of my normal activities, minimal though they were. Faced with a liberty to call my own, with no attachments, my spirit failed. The life I had now threatened to be empty, for those unknown others, in whom I had once placed my nebulous hopes, would prove too insubstantial to fill the abyss that had opened so suddenly under my feet.

I should have welcomed a dream, though I could not hope for a dream as radiant as that strange dream which had seemed to me so significant. Its significance had proved elusive, even fallacious. It had had to do with hope, with a promise of fulfilment. Now it was clear that I should have to proceed step by cautious step. I could anticipate my faltering progress, my resigned determination. Even the luxury of sleep would perhaps—almost certainly—be denied me. As I felt my eyes finally close it was not relief that I felt but a sensation of falling, and the threat of a fear from which there might be no release.

8

'MY DEAR FRANÇOISE,' I WROTE. 'AS YOU MAY HAVE SUR-
mised I am in London. I had to return suddenly: my mother
died, with what seems to me equal suddenness. People have assured me that I have been spared much, in that I did not have
to witness a long illness, but I doubt if there is a great deal to
choose between one way of death and another. As a daughter,
and an only daughter, you can imagine how I feel. I should
have written earlier but there has been a lot to do, although we
were a very small, not to say nonexistent, family. I shall stay
here until I have made all the arrangements, and paid all the
bills. I shall return to Paris to collect my things, and may stay
for a while. I have not yet decided where to live, and intend to
make no hasty decisions. Naturally I shall look in at the library
in order to see you, and hope that we can have lunch or coffee,
as we usually did. I should welcome your sensible advice, not
that I ever took it, but there is a shortage of it here and I find
its absence rather depressing. I shall send this to the flat—I can't

quite bring myself to send it to the library—and look forward to seeing you. No need to reply to this. *Avec toute mon amitié,* Emma.'

'Dear Michael,' I then wrote. 'I can never thank you enough for your kindness on that terrible evening. It seems, in retrospect, like a bad dream from which I have not yet woken. I say bad dream rather than nightmare because its effects have proved so long-lasting. One wakes abruptly from a nightmare and recognizes it for what it is, but I can expect no such relief from my present situation, which is principally one of strange haunted drowsiness. I think of you often, not only in connection with that night, but rather as I remember you, walking, always thoughtfully, and usually on your own, but sometimes on a Sunday, when I was included. We shall meet again—or shall we? The thought has suddenly struck me that I might not return to Paris, although obviously I shall have to come back to pick up my things. I have a feeling of finality, of endings, which I do not quite understand. Clever people, unlike myself, seem to recognize when a friendship has run its course, and everyone knows, however reluctantly, when a love affair is over, but to say goodbye to an enthusiasm is mysterious. I had persuaded myself, only a short time ago, that I could live in Paris, pick up some sort of work, translating or even teaching, and manage an existence devoid of formal obligations. Now I see that what I am describing was a sort of youthfulness which has now come to an end. Frankly, I do not know where to live, nor does it much matter. And in this new mood of unadulterated realism it seems that all my arrangements, even my friendships, were flimsy. This new realism reminds me of my initial bewilderment at being so unattached, so careful, and so uncomfortable. This was a singularly poor apprenticeship, and my researches, though painstaking, were always this side of enthusiasm. But I know that I shall always remember certain Sunday afternoons that we spent together, wandering, like any other couple, in public gardens, in the early days of a spring that now seems far distant. These walks were without emotional significance, and perhaps all the better for that. There never were two such silent companions, but I think we understood each other as well as we could without the benefit of conversation. Thank you for your company. I am of course assuming that you will stay in Paris, and hope that this reaches you. There is no need to reply. If you want to you can always write to me here, and I hope that you will. Ever, Emma.'

I knew that I might not see him again: this had become clear as my letter took shape. The innocence of that friendship pertained to youth, almost to childhood, and that time was at an end. My heaviness of spirit, and of body, was that of a reluctant adult, beset with adult arrangements, adult decisions. It was only when I heard the sound of my uncle's key in the door that I regressed: a true adult, such as I thought I had become, would have asked for the key to be given back, but as he was striving to be nice it would have been ungracious to do so. He would

look in, always unannounced, to see if I were all right and, having decided that I was, leave with a sense of duty done. He was
the single reason for my entertaining the possibility of remov-
ing to Paris, but I preferred to postpone any decision of a far-
reaching nature until I was clear in my mind, and could face
the future, my future, without assistance, for I knew there would
be none. I should have preferred to have the future decided for
me by others, even though I knew that few people volunteer
for such a task. I saw the point of families, of marriage; I wondered how long I was expected to manage on my own. This
was my most unsettling dilemma, and in its wake came the
conviction that my mother's loneliness, if loneliness was what
it was, might have taken the form of an unfinished internal debate on the nature of self-sufficiency, on its limits, and on the
character requirements necessary for a good outcome. It was a
debate she had had to have with herself, as I should, and if I
were not extremely vigilant I might run the risk of living her
life all over again. The prospect frightened me very much.

Apart from these considerations I found myself oddly in-
attentive to the business of ordinary life. My circumstances lent
themselves to this passivity: I was warm, I was comfortable,
I was undisturbed. I had learned that I had inherited some
money from my mother, who had been saving on my behalf.
This both consoled and saddened me—consoled me in so far
as it reminded me of her love, and saddened me because that
love had been so wistful, so undemonstrative. There was no

reason I could see why I should not remain here, but there was a factor I could not ignore: I was becoming increasingly unwilling to leave the flat. I made a few hasty purchases first thing in the morning and ate what I had bought without interest or appetite. I marvelled at my insouciance in the cafés and the occasional restaurant I had frequented in Paris and knew that I could not replicate it here. I preferred my own company, my own solitude, although efforts had been made to reduce that solitude to what others considered manageable proportions. Friends I had not seen since college, and who were now married, urged me to attend their dinner parties, dismissing my reclusion as unhealthy, unseemly, something no reasonable person could contemplate. So far I had resisted these kind invitations, but the perceived danger of even greater isolation would eventually oblige me, with a heavy heart, to comply. I had been in London for three weeks, nearly a month, and I would end up doing what others wanted me to do, because that was what people such as myself usually did. It was just that late evenings, in strange houses, held no appeal; moreover they would interfere with a particularly precious time, when I renounced the day and surrendered to the dark. I went to bed earlier and earlier, and lay there waiting to fall asleep. The dread that I had experienced on that first night had not disappeared, but now I knew that it would always be with me, like some chronic weakness, a bad knee, say, or a blocked sinus, and that I could and should live with it. It is perhaps significant that I found waking much more problematic, part of the inevitable decision-making from which I was not to be relieved, however many invitations came my way, however much advice I appeared to welcome. My real deliverance was nowhere in sight.

What finally decided me was the beautiful weather, which I could no longer ignore. Every morning the sun rose into a cloudless sky; a dawn mist would leave droplets of moisture on blades of grass which emerged with almost pre-Raphaelite intensity. After completing my early purchases I went home, intending to do something useful, but would be drawn to the window to contemplate the brilliance of the day. It was the light that delivered me from my torpor, and although imprisoned in a strange idleness I could see that action was called for. I was as ready as I ever should be to go back to Paris, and, more difficult, to link up with my two friends. I knew that we should all be constrained, and that the limits of our friendship, now that there was no longer continuity to sustain it, would soon be reached. I saw that habit, and more than habit, proximity, can create a sort of friendship that is in fact not intimate, and wondered if my letters had presumed too much, revealed too much, or, worse, reminded the recipients that I had needs that they were required to address, when in fact it was in both their natures to be massively self-absorbed. It was entirely possible that they were not where I expected them to be, that the habits which I took for granted had already been cancelled, in which case I should merely collect my things and avoid making contact altogether. There would be no need to explain this; they both had my address should they wish to get in touch. In my worst moments I imagined them puzzling over my name: Emma? Emma who? This I put down to the general nervousness which had overtaken me whenever I left the flat. That nervousness increased when I booked my ticket.

Paris was subtly different, or maybe I had changed, grown accustomed to birdsong and small front gardens and women impatient with their lot and a populace hypnotized by what it watched on television. Yet my room in the hotel remained its own uncommunicative self. I picked up my briefcase and made my way to the library. Françoise's eyes widened. I was right; she had not expected to see me again. Nevertheless she pointed to her watch, and then beyond the door, and indicated that I was to meet her at our usual café round the corner. I almost wished that I had come and gone in a spirit of secrecy which would have served me better and spared my friends embarrassment. No one knows how to behave in the presence of death, and Françoise, for all her boldness, was no exception. She regarded me curiously, as if I might manifest worrying symptoms, almost warning me not to bring my concerns into her life, precariously balanced as it was between her mother's will and her own. I knew that I must exert tact, and so I told her that she looked well, and that I was glad to see her, however briefly.

'You're not staying, then?' she asked.

'Oh, no. There's really no reason for me to do so.'

'How will you live now?'

'Oh, much as usual, I suppose. If you're ever in London you must come and stay. There's plenty of room in the flat.' There was a pause, almost but not quite awkward. 'How's your mother?' I asked.

She shrugged. 'You've met my mother. Incidentally, you made a very good impression.' She lit a cigarette, something I had not seen her do before. 'My mother is odious,' she said calmly.

'I found her rather impressive.'

'Oh, she is certainly that.'

Another pause. 'And Jean-Charles?'

'Fortunately he and his mother are away. They have a small property near Montpellier. Most people are away, or going away. It's Easter, after all.'

'I hadn't noticed.'

'You should take a holiday, Emma. After such a difficult time . . .'

How does one survive without a mother was what she wanted to ask me, yet she was fearful of doing so, anxious not to touch on the great drama of her life, a drama that would overshadow any that she might encounter with lovers or eventually her husband.

'Will you marry him?' I asked, conscious that this was none of my business, and no longer very interested.

She ignored this. 'What you should do is come away with

me this weekend. Yes, why not do that? My mother would be delighted.'

'I should be getting back. . . .'

'I'll pick you up at your hotel, if you like. Or better, collect me at the library tomorrow evening. I'll drive us down. The evenings are light now.'

'Yes, indeed,' I said politely. 'Are you sure?'

'Quite sure.' She picked up her bag. 'Until tomorrow evening, then.'

I watched her leave, sorry to see her go, although our meeting had not been satisfactory. I wondered if this had been my fault, if I had been less than correct in broaching matters which had once been frankly discussed. Suddenly I wanted to be at home, undisturbed, above all unquestioned. I did not want to be a weekend guest. The invitations I had refused in London would have been less wearisome than the formality I should have to observe with her mother, if I were not to betray my sadness. And yet it would have been impolite to refuse, though a more competent person would have done so at once. My very politeness had, once again, let me down.

I spent the day aimlessly wandering, visiting one or two bookshops, longing for the evening when I might see Michael. But when evening finally came there was no sign of him. This I put down to forgetfulness on his part, nothing more sinister. I went to bed early, as I usually did, but regretted my soft bed and slept badly. I woke in a fever of impatience to get the day, the weekend, over, so that I could go back to being obscure and undiscovered. I squandered the morning and much of the afternoon. I presented myself at the library almost angrily. Not only did I not want this, but Françoise, and even more so her mother, would not want it either. We drove down almost in silence.

Yet the beauty of the house conquered me once again. It was flushed with pink in the light of a dying sun, its doors open to let in the last of the light. Mme Desnoyers was nowhere to be seen, but her high heels could be heard on various surfaces—tiles, wood—and her appearance would be signalled by the usual dramatic sound effects. When she did appear she greeted me with a kindness for which I was unprepared. So unprepared was I for this that the tears I had not shed since my mother's death made their way down my cheeks and grew more abundant as I tried to check them. She surveyed me almost thoughtfully, then took me in her arms. '*Pauvre petite,*' she said, and turned to Françoise. That is how a daughter should behave, was her unspoken message. Will you ever be of this quality?

After that it was bearable. I succumbed to what was already a routine: the airtight bedroom, the lukewarm food, the laconic exchanges between the two women. In the absence of her adversary, Mme de Lairac, Mme Desnoyers seemed homelier, less effortful. Her ambitions for the moment laid aside, she almost regressed to whatever had been her original status. There were even signs of carelessness in her less rigid posture, her worn jacket. On the other hand, and possibly not unconnected, her sawing asthmatic breath was no longer noticeable. She was comfortable as she was.

After dinner we watched television, the same American serial that all England had been watching.

'*Pouah!*' she uttered. '*Ils sont mal élevés, ces gens.*'

It was that disgusted '*Pouah!*' that underlined the resemblance between mother and daughter. I smiled; Françoise did the same, but with a certain constraint. What we had been watching was a scene of more or less unbridled lust in which two extremely glamorous people were conducting their courtship in a setting of fabulous luxury. I saw, with some surprise, that Françoise was inclined to take this rather more seriously than I would have suspected. Was this, then, her ideal? A total escape from everything she had been brought up to observe? Would she have wanted this surfeit of worldly goods? Would she have made her peace with them, even embraced the vulgarity that was, if anything, an added temptation? Mme Desnoyers intuited this, though gave no sign of having done so. But her breathing became noisier, and when she switched off the television Françoise did not protest.

We were in her bedroom, no television being admitted in the grand downstairs rooms, though her bedroom was grand enough. Grand, but untidy, a chair pushed away from a small desk, a cupboard door not quite closed. The huge bed seemed inappropriate to one so obviously celibate. The bed, in fact, belonged in the sort of scene we had been watching rather than as part of the life so carefully cultivated here. *'Maman!'* warned Françoise.

'Yes,' she said. 'I am tired. We must all go to bed. *Bonne nuit, mes filles.'*

I never forgot that. It seemed like a sign that I still existed as a daughter, that my daughterly condition was once more acceptable. I was so grateful to her that I kissed her, which was a grave mistake. She stiffened; it was after all for her to kiss me, if she wished, not the other way round. But this was somehow part of living in France, doing the infinitesimal wrong thing. It was part of the barbarism of being English. As I retired, slightly shamefaced, I realized that I was irreducibly English. And yet I was beguiled, as an outsider, by a way of life that would, I knew, continue to exert its fascination. The experience had been decisive: I had been included. What was more, I had given some sort of satisfaction, if only by virtue of my naïveté.

Françoise confirmed this as we were driving back to Paris. 'You seem to have a good effect on my mother,' she said. 'You don't know how rare that is. When I went in to her this morning she told me to tell you to come again. Will you come again, Emma?'

'Oh, yes,' I assured her, knowing that my assent could be easily overlooked. 'I'd love to.'

9

ON LOOKING THROUGH MY TEXT I WAS AGREEABLY SUR-
prised to find it quite interesting: my chapter on Le Nôtre
was, I thought, on the right lines. I had planned to spend the
morning doing this; in fact it took less than an hour. When the
telephone rang I was almost grateful, less so when the caller
turned out to be Sarah Buchanan, now Cartwright, whom I
had known at college, though Sarah always made it seem like
school. She was a bustling insensitive girl whom I had never
much liked, although she appeared to consider us firm friends.
She regarded me with some condescension, both for living at
home with my mother and devoting my time to work of a not
immediately relevant nature. 'It's not going to save the planet, is
it?' she quipped when informed of my choice of subject, and
laughed at her own sally. I was reminded, as were we all, that
she was engaged to a medical student, and thus doing her bit
for humanity. She tolerated me as a rare example of one so
backward that I could only benefit from her guidance. As I was

slightly frightened of her I did my best to defuse her quips without actually giving offence. I never considered her a true friend, not knowing that true friends are exceedingly rare, but simply as part of the context from which I had emerged and which now seemed infinitely distant. At the same time I recognized that it was kind of her to telephone. I was a little bored—a sign of recovery, perhaps—and still uncertain whether I should stay in London or not. France had treated me kindly, in an unobtrusive way, and Michael was still there. I was unhappy that I had missed him on my last visit. This was unfinished business, and I wanted to talk to him. Indeed he was the only one to whom I did want to talk. As a solitary he would have understood me perfectly; more than that, his very solitariness gave him intellectual prestige, like the desert fathers who were assumed to have gained wisdom from their limiting circumstances without doing too much to give an account of themselves, content to be pictured contemplating a skull in many an Old Master painting.

'Listen,' said Sarah. 'I won't ask you again. Dinner on Friday. There's someone I want you to meet.'

These words struck terror into my heart. I knew her range of acquaintances, an even heartier reflection of her own nature. Her fiancé, now her husband, and now a doctor, was her exact equivalent. How lucky they were! Yet I did not envy her, nor did I question her choice. This was a Darwinian partnership, a blueprint for survival which one could not question.

And they were the fittest, no doubt of that. If they made one feel lacking in evolutionary potential, that was hardly their fault. And yet the air of triumph that was Sarah's outstanding characteristic could not be explained away entirely by the powers of love.

'I really don't think . . .'

'Now, don't let me down,' she menaced. 'You know where we are. Dorset Square, eight o'clock.'

Eight o'clock was when I sometimes wondered whether it was too early to go to bed. It was only on reflecting that this behaviour was aberrant that I thanked her and said that nonetheless she should not expect me to fall in with her plans.

She laughed. 'France hasn't changed you much, has it?'

'I've enjoyed myself enormously,' I said primly. 'In fact I'm thinking of going back.'

'You must tell us all what you've been up to,' she said. 'Don't be late. Eight o'clock. No need to dress.'

Until that moment I had not given a thought to what I was to wear. Now I was doomed to shop for something. This would no doubt fill the day, and it was too fine a morning to be spent in this manner. But I remembered my shame at being found wanting by Mme Desnoyers and her guests (and perhaps by Françoise as well), and resolved to do better. I preferred to be unobtrusive, anonymous, to eat in a familiar café where a mere nod of the head was understood as a means of communication, a brief greeting enough to establish recognition. Now

I should have to dress up and be on display, patronage having been advertised in advance. Harrods might have something, I thought vaguely. Then perhaps I could eat lunch out. I needed to be reintroduced to the outside world and thought this as good a way as any.

In fact the day served to establish the distance between the present and my past existence. So disconcerting was this distance that I resolved to embark on some further study, knowing that I would be undisturbed in this endeavour and perhaps succumbing to the delusion that I would always be young, a beginner, an apprentice. I did not crave the company of Sarah and her like. The women in Harrods seemed confident and purposeful, and there were no men at all. I spent far too much money on a dress I was quite sure I should never wear again, though it was pretty enough and fitted perfectly. In the mirror I looked like a child dressed for a birthday party, and was shocked by my own unworldliness. This perhaps was the obverse of a life of study, this fear of social situations in which I should be found wanting, having nothing to offer in the way of gossip or news or plans, too obviously ignorant of the game to be played, the prizes to be won. The person whom Sarah wanted me to meet could be dealt with quite easily. I was quite expert in this matter, having been the focus of unwanted attention on several occasions in Paris. But there it had had little to do with formal introductions, and not very much with social standing. I knew that Jean-Charles de Lairac would have indicated his intentions had his mother not been present. In comparison with what that would have entailed, Sarah's friend would pose no problem.

Nevertheless I was glad that I was dressed up when I was introduced to the two other couples, both married, the women rather more impressive than the men. They were named as Susie and Alison, both of whom, I knew, would recognize the provenance and price of my outfit, which looked fussy compared with their sleek trouser suits. The husbands, conferring among themselves, were, I supposed, doctors, as was my intended. 'Philip will be a little late,' explained Sarah. 'He had to go back to the hospital. He said to go ahead without him.'

'Oh, Philip,' smiled Susie or Alison. 'Always impossible.'

'Yes, indeed. I was lucky to get hold of him at all.'

I was relieved. The main feature, which they were all there to witness, might not take place at all. With that in mind I was prepared to play my part with as much goodwill as I could muster.

'Of course, he hasn't been the same since his wife left him. Do bring your glasses. I hope you're ready to eat.'

All these people were prosperous, it seemed. There was some sort of help in the kitchen. Everyone but myself had traded up. The talk was of property prices, and holidays, past, present, and to come. Their principal occupation seemed to be taking holidays; nowhere was too distant, no terrain too difficult. Susie and David went skiing. Alison and Jim had recently been trekking in Nepal.

'You must be awfully fit,' I ventured, sincerely impressed.

'You ought to do something like that,' said Sarah. 'Do you more good than all that studying.'

'What exactly do you do?' enquired Alison, the trekker.

I was spared the possible embarrassment of a reply by the irruption of a harassed-looking man whom they all greeted joyously as 'Philip!'

'Sorry, sorry,' he replied, with an attempt at breeziness which seemed suitable for the occasion, though it did not quite eliminate the heaviness of his features.

'Sit down, sit down. I hope you're hungry,' said Sarah. 'Though it must be spoiled by now.'

I felt for her then, for her energy, her desire. All this was imprinted in her gestures. And the food was indeed excellent.

'Sorry,' he said again, and sat down humbly. All watched him eat. He seemed to be something of a celebrity, or at least someone whose company was something to be cherished. He answered questions while forking food into his mouth. Even the men looked on approvingly.

I studied this man whom Sarah had produced for my benefit, though from the look on her face, just as much for hers. Large, rumpled, and perhaps as uncomfortable as I was. A brief look in my direction had identified me as his partner. The breeziness, no doubt his professional manner, lapsed from time to time into a sombre-seeming passivity. The breeziness was resumed manfully as plates of food were placed before him in quick succession. He seemed anxious to get the business of refuelling over as quickly as possible.

'You probably had no lunch,' said Sarah fondly.

'Busy day,' he replied, rousing himself from a momentary lapse in attention. 'Philip Hudson,' he said, looking at me properly for the first time. 'Emma Roberts,' I replied.

'Oh!' said Sarah, clapping her hand to her forehead. 'I forgot to introduce you.'

Philip Hudson retrieved his social manners. 'Delicious,' he pronounced. Then, digestion having begun its work, he fell back into a silence which seemed to be more natural to him. The look in his eyes had something mournful about it.

'Coffee next door,' announced Sarah.

In the sitting room I was able to observe him more closely. He did not seem the kind of man to entertain one with anecdotes about his holidays. On the contrary, he seemed serious, weighty, no trace of his bustling entry. His hand idled with his coffee cup until Sarah took it from him.

'Are you very tired?' she enquired, as his silence deepened.

'Well, as I said, busy day. A full list.' He glanced at his watch. 'If you don't mind, Sarah, I'll be on my way fairly soon. I'm scheduled for eight o'clock tomorrow morning.'

'We'll let you go this time,' she said, disappointed but brave. 'But only if you promise to give us a proper evening very soon.'

'Too kind, my dear. Can I give anyone a lift?' He glanced in my direction.

'Actually, Sarah, if you don't mind, I'll make a move myself.'

'Oh, Emma, there's no need. Well, if you're sure . . .'

'It's been lovely,' I assured her. 'I'll ring you before I go back.'

'Back where?'

'To Paris. One or two things to clear up.'

She let me go with what seemed like genuine regret. Dr Hudson was retained for a multiplicity of leave-takings. Finally we were in the street. The sudden silence, and the beautiful evening, or rather night, calmed us both. I felt as if I had been away from home for weeks, though, strangely, I was not tired. I was well-disposed towards Dr Hudson by virtue of the fact that he was a man who knew how to make a quick getaway, and to take me with him. At the end of the street leading to Sarah's flat lay freedom, and with it lights, passing cars, the lit window of a café. That the café was filled with solitary-looking people endeared it to me. I might, in other circumstances, have been one of them.

'I forgot to bring the car. Or rather I decided not to. I can't give you a lift after all.'

'I'll get a cab,' I assured him. 'In fact I think I'll walk a bit. It's such a lovely evening.'

'I'll walk with you. Actually I live quite near. York Street. I often walk home from the hospital, Chelsea. And from Harley Street, of course.'

'You're a doctor?'

'Surgeon. Most of the people I meet are unconscious, properly anaesthetized. Saves a lot of idle chatter.'

'And yet you turned out for a dinner party.'

'It was either that or a takeaway.' We walked on. 'And what do you do?' he said finally.

'Nothing, really.'

'You were described to me as a distinguished scholar.'

'That was nice of them, but far from true, I'm afraid. I live alone. My mother died recently and I came home to settle things. I'd been away, you see.'

'Yes, I'd picked that up.'

'I suppose this is home now but I find it very disconcerting. Everyone seems so well-off. And it's a different sort of conversation one has here. Full of jokes.'

'That may be defensive.'

'Why?'

'People don't trust seriousness. It worries them.'

'I find jokiness far more worrying. Perhaps I am ill-equipped for it. I work alone, you see,' I went on, suddenly anxious to give an account of myself. 'I sit in a library and work on my book. At least it's not a book yet, but I think it might become one. . . .'

'You'll find that everyone in England is writing a book.'

'My book—if it becomes one—would be very boring. It's about classical garden design.'

'I have rather a nice garden.'

'In York Street?'

'No. I have a house in Winchelsea.'

I gave up. There was no point in going on. Besides, he had lapsed into his intermittent state of absence. I assumed that he had more important matters on his mind. Or maybe he was anxious to get rid of this tedious obligation to be polite. We were both uncomfortable.

'I'm sorry,' he said. 'I'm no good at this sort of thing.'

'I don't like it much either.' I saw no harm in speaking my mind out here, in the calming night air. I had not forgotten the mild pleasure of walking with a man.

'Do you mind living alone?'

'No, not really. It's just that . . .'

'I live alone myself. My wife left me, you see. They probably told you that. She was exasperated by the hours I kept. Also she liked company. She was—is—very beautiful.'

'And family?'

'One son. A junior doctor in Liverpool. I don't see much

of him. He lets himself into the house from time to time and goes to bed, exhausted. We don't talk much. But we get on pretty well.'

'You're proud of him.'

'I am, yes.'

'People assume that I'm lonely. That's why they ask me to dinner.'

'Same here, I expect.'

'And are you lonely?'

'No,' he said shortly, cutting off that line of enquiry.

'I'm sorry. I shouldn't have asked. That sort of question seems taboo here. In Paris it's considered a legitimate preamble to a far-reaching discussion.'

'God, how awful.'

'I can see a cab,' I said.

'Do forgive me. As I said, I'm no good at this.'

'Oh, please.' I was struck by a sudden disappointment. The weekend was approaching, was nearly upon us, a laborious Saturday and an empty Sunday, which even this newfound English joviality could not combat. I was still subject to the memory of other Sundays, but I saw that I had built up an illusion of true partnership which had nothing to sustain it. That peculiar charm of mutual silence would not stand up to scrutiny, nor could it be conveyed. The roses would now be in bloom at Malmaison, I thought with a pang. Mothers-in-law would be taken out for their weekly treat. The children would be paci-

fied with ice cream. All would be well-behaved, pacific, ready
for the next working day. And I felt part of that petit-bourgeois
world, protective of it.

'I hate the thought of Sunday,' I heard myself saying.

'I don't much like weekends,' he said. 'I usually look in to
the hospital. Or go out to lunch.'

'Yes, I suppose you have many invitations.'

'No, I mean I go to a restaurant. Or an hotel. I'm no
cook.'

'Neither am I.'

'Perhaps you'd like to lunch one Sunday?'

'Yes, I'd like that.'

'Sooner the better. What about this Sunday?'

'Fine.'

'Hyde Park Hotel, twelve-thirty. That suit you? I'll get
that cab. You must be tired with all this walking.'

Little did he know. We had merely reached Marble Arch;
had it not been for the no-man's-land of the park I should have
carried on.

'My name is Philip,' he said, shutting the door of the cab.
'Until Sunday, then. Good night.'

In the taxi I regretted the streets, dark, but with a summer
openness, no thought of danger, no feeling of distress, I regretted the walk, uncomfortable though it had been—but then the
whole evening had been uncomfortable. Sarah would no doubt
preempt my telephone call, anxious to know how we had got

on. There was an unseemliness about such obvious match-making. The man Hudson had shown commendable restraint on the whole. I should probably not see him again, nor need to. There remained the problem of lunch two days ahead. I did not have a telephone number for him. Sarah could supply one, but that might encourage speculation. I was not at home with these manoeuvres. I was not even at home in the flat, which seemed newly strange, dim after Sarah's bright lights, silent after the conversation. No sane person would exchange its comforts for that hotel room. It was perhaps no more than a question of habit, or rather of usage. In those modest surroundings I knew my own mind, had achieved a certain mild autonomy. Here I was lost among strangers whom I could never please. Here was exile, but perhaps reality, a reality with which I should have to come to terms.

10

'YOU SEEM IN BETTER SPIRITS TODAY,' SAID PHILIP HUD-
son, as we ate cold salmon in the Hyde Park Hotel. 'Perhaps
you were not at your best the other evening.'

'I don't think I have a best. Better, perhaps, but not best.
Yes, I do feel better today. This is so nice. It was kind of you to
suggest it. Do you really come here at the weekends? On your
own?'

'Yes. Being on one's own is quite an education. One sees
more people but knows hardly anyone. And if one stays at
home the day lacks a focus. One is inclined to read too many
newspapers. Anyway, I never think of my house as "home". I
think of it as the house, or my house.'

'That is how I think of my flat. I never say I'm going
home. I say I'm going back to the flat.'

A waiter removed our plates.

'Do you imagine an ideal home? Somewhere you long to
be? I sometimes think I could be happier somewhere else. Not

happy, mark you: happier. I see some quite ordinary house and think, yes, something like that. Maybe it's only a detail, a curtain blowing at an upstairs window. . . .'

'My house suited me well enough when my family lived there. My wife. My boy, when he was little.'

'What is his name?'

'Mark. My wife called him Markie. Do smoke if you want to.'

'I don't, thank you. There's a house I visit in France occasionally. Not that I think of living there . . . I suppose one is tempted by other lives. It's like what you were saying about seeing people and not knowing them. One is always on the lookout for something or someone. Not necessarily romantic, just an indicator of change. Will you stay in York Street, or move somewhere else?'

'No need. It's a decent enough house. You'll see it one day. Today, if you've got the time. We'll have coffee there.'

'I suppose it's always easier to stay than to leave.'

'Ah. Leaving home: the great drama of our lives.'

'Maybe it gets better as one gets older.'

'No, worse. Everything gets worse as one gets older. Shall we go?'

I studied him as covertly as possible in this unusual proximity. He seemed twice my age, even more, but this was due less to his appearance than to his latent melancholy, which rose to the surface, always without warning, as it did now. He carried it off but did not attempt to disguise it. If anything it added to his distinction, which was conveyed largely by his height and bulk: here, his appearance signalled, was a man of consequence. This did much to compensate for scanty hair and commonplace features. I had no difficulty in accepting him as someone with arcane gifts which I should not be obliged to understand. There was no small talk possible; in any case he did not seem to deal in small talk. Everything about him was weighty, including what he had to say. This was a great relief to me; to my surprise I found it easy to fill the gaps. This meeting, which could have been extremely awkward, was proving a success, or at least not an outright failure. If we were ever to meet again I need have no anxieties about my appearance, to which he seemed completely indifferent, or my general appeal, relevance, or desirability, to which he was equally immune. It was a relief to be beyond the range of feeling, for however brief an interlude. Everything seemed acceptably impersonal: the high-ceilinged restaurant, the view of the park beyond the windows, the unobtrusive service. I could see why he chose to eat here. I had originally thought his choice eccentric. Now I saw it as entirely commendable.

'Your book is finished?' he queried as we sat in the cab.

'No. At least it is almost finished as a thesis, but is far from being a book.' This reflection slightly clouded my appreciation of the day. If I intended to go ahead with this project—and I had few other calls on my time and attention—I should need to revisit some of the sites to which I had given my attention, and I discovered that I was no longer eager to do so. I also saw that my material was thin in places (the section on Villandry came to mind) and must be radically restructured. This would mean some travelling, none of it arduous, but unwelcome for other reasons. It was not merely a question of displacement, though that came into it; it had to do with a nascent longing for a less isolated life. I had hitherto functioned well enough in solitude, but I knew that I had little hope of attaining Philip Hudson's stoicism. For that was what was needed, however one compensated oneself with civilized pursuits. Solitude may favour study but is insufficient if one's aim is creative thinking. And one might encounter an inconvenient longing for company, intimacy, and the anticipation of similar delights. That was the mantra of the times: entitlement. I knew that however pleasant this day had been, much was left out. Politeness had kept us in order, but prolonged politeness might prove unsustainable. I wished the afternoon to progress, but in some unexpected fashion. And when it ended, as it must do, after more polite exchanges, there was the less companionable future to be negotiated. And that future must be invested with a significance which for the moment entirely escaped me.

'You have a young man, I take it?' he enquired. He seemed bulkier getting out of the taxi, perhaps regretting this invitation. I should have left him at the hotel. I thought with some embarrassment of my obvious willingness to accompany him, and determined to leave as soon as I could.

'Yes, I have a young man. At least I think I do.'

'Why only think?'

'We are close in several unspoken ways. We are both self-sufficient. . . .' My voice trailed off. 'I mean we are very alike. We like the same things.'

But those things now seemed insubstantial. Those humble Sunday afternoons were, perhaps, a little quaint. We were spectators rather than participants, far removed from those families which we observed with such approval. Michael had seemed as orphaned as myself, and yet I knew that he had parents in Oxford, and, for all I knew, a perfectly normal family life. Whatever had served to make him so unsociable was not likely to be divulged; our conversation, sparse as it was, did not explore such fundamental matters. I missed him as I might miss a familiar. If we seemed to be related it was because that was how we wished to be. In that sense I should always love him, although knowing that our relationship, though close, was in some ways fortuitous, that it left many questions unanswered, and many roles unfilled.

'You are very fortunate, then. Compatibility is vital. One ignores its absence at one's peril. My wife and I had wildly divergent tastes. I ignored that too, thinking I could make life pleasant for her.'

'I'm sure you did.'

'Yes, I thought so too. Or hoped so.'

'When did you part?'

'Three years ago. This is my house. I'll make coffee.'

'And then I'll leave you. I've probably ruined your quiet day. You've been very kind.'

'A pleasure. Ah!' he said, seeing a set of keys on a small table in the hall. 'My son is here.'

'Would you like me to go? If you want to spend time with him . . .'

'No, not at all. He'll be asleep anyway. They work them so hard these days. No need to whisper. He'll be dead to the world.'

I took the opportunity of his absence in the kitchen to look round the room from which he was anxious to escape. I understood his reluctance to spend a Sunday afternoon here. It appeared to be half-furnished: perhaps his wife had carried off the more attractive pieces. The house was handsome enough in its flat-fronted way from the outside, but gloomy within. Dark stairs led up to this first-floor drawing room, which seemed redolent of absence. Three widely spaced armchairs and a small round table were marooned on a hardwood floor, throwing into stark relief a set of unembellished shelves. Dull striped curtains, of an obviously expensive material, obscured much of the light, although the day had been sunny. Now I was aware of a chill which seemed not so much physical as emotional. Yet

he was not obviously deprived; his conversation had if anything been bracing. I thought that he had made a respectable
job of his semi-widowed state, and gave no sign of torment,
though that might have existed. It was not a room in which
one was tempted to move about. Once assigned to a chair one
would be inclined to wait there for further orders, as I did
now.

'I seem to have taken up a good part of your afternoon,' I
said, when he returned with a tray.

'Not at all. I have enjoyed your company.'

This sounded so final that I took it as a sign for me to
leave. But I was sufficiently afflicted by the gloom of the room
to wonder how he would spend the rest of the day.

'Will you go to the hospital this afternoon?' I asked. 'Or
what's left of it.'

'No, not if Mark is here. Though I expect he'll go and
visit his mother this evening.'

'Does she live near here?'

'St John's Wood.' This was offered curtly, as if her place
should be kept concealed.

Here was a man wounded by love and not knowing how
to recover. He was also angry, but thought it a matter of honour to conceal this too. I thought him intriguing, rather ad
mirable, though that glimpse of sore feelings—the flat in St
John's Wood—did not do him justice. I preferred him stoical,
calm, world-weary; presumably this was easier to achieve in the

Hyde Park Hotel than in this room which signalled his aban-
donment. He seemed to feel this too, and may have wished me
out of the way.

'I'll leave you now,' I said. 'Thank you so much for lunch.
I really enjoyed seeing you again.' We both rose. 'If I might just
use your bathroom . . .'

'Upstairs. Second door on the left.'

I walked up the stairs as unobtrusively as I could. The
doors on the right were open. Through one I caught sight
of a rumpled bed, and on it the body of a young man. Unable to prevent myself from doing so I tiptoed in. He—Mark,
presumably—was fast asleep. His sleep seemed to me excep-
tional, total, his arms flung out, his face classical in its emptiness.
For a moment I contemplated him, as Psyche once contemplated Cupid, raising her lamp, willing him not to wake and
witness her transgression. At the sight of his surrendered nakedness I saw what had been missing from my life. It was another
coup de foudre, information received, though not knowingly
given. My shock was unwitnessed, but perhaps all the more
profound for that reason. I would have welcomed some sign of
comprehension, even of willingness to talk, but I was alone in
this discovery, and perhaps one always is. I could appreciate the
virtues of taciturnity, as I could with Michael, but now I had
seen what was infinitely more desirable: the arms flung out, the
expression of satiety. It was only sleep, I reminded myself, but I
did not see how anyone could have enough of it. I walked

steadily down the stairs and back into the room, where Philip
Hudson stood, waiting for me to leave.

'Do you want a cab?' he asked.

'No, no, I'll walk. I hope you have a pleasant evening.'

He handed me a card. 'I hope you'll get in touch. If you'd
write your telephone number down for me?'

As I did I could hear sounds of stirring, of footsteps, from
the upper room.

'Ah,' he said, with a smile that made his heavy features
briefly attractive. 'He's awake.' He glanced at his watch. 'Just
time to discuss his plans before he goes off.'

'His plans?'

'He intends to join Médecins sans Frontières. As I should
have done at his age. Live all you can, as Henry James said.'

'Oh, yes. Goodbye.'

'Goodbye. I hope we may meet again?'

'I hope so too.'

This was an alliance to which any sensible woman might
consent, had she not experienced the sudden illumination of
understanding what would be missed, and if she were excep-
tionally sensible, in spite of that. He felt it too; I knew that,
though I scarcely knew him. It would be an alliance in which
only basic information would be shared, in which concealment
would be taken for granted. It was the sort of alliance I enjoyed
with Michael, precious in itself, but no longer adequate. In a
bleak world, a world deprived of emotional comfort, this might

suffice. It would be calm, undemanding, like those Sunday afternoons at Malmaison, at Saint-Cloud. We had been planning to see the roses at Bagatelle before I had had to come away. Now it seemed to me that I had been away too long, had let a fatal interval elapse since our last meeting. He must have got used to my absence. I should have to get in touch, telephone the hotel, leave a message if he were not there. He was my defence against loneliness. Yet at the same time I thought back to the figure on the bed and acknowledged my lack of joy.

I had tried to live my life according to the classical ideal, that of order and control and self-mastery. That was the principle that imposed itself on the unruliness of nature in the shape of paths, parterres, rigorous right angles. Now I saw that such symmetry was only temporary, and that at some point nature would resume the upper hand. For nature I should henceforth understand the body. To faint, to weep, however briefly, was to be under the command of the body. And this was dangerous. I thought with horror of my instinctive, almost automatic desire to touch that sleeper. I had not done so. But I had walked into his room . . . Now, once again, I saw the virtue in those classical principles. In the end only restraint stood up to scrutiny. An alliance based on friendship was more reliable than love. Yet love remains the ideal. Live all you can.

I had reached the bottom of Baker Street without knowing how I had got there. I thought I should walk home, or rather 'home'. The evenings were light now, though darkness might have been more appropriate. I walked in a straight line through the park, which was now emptying; few couples lingered, though those that did so were intent on each other, invulnerable in each other's company. I continued walking. I was not anxious for the day to end. The very real pleasure of the occasion, the meal, the visit, had been mitigated by what I had seen, and felt. From that, I knew, there was no going back. Our minds, our feelings can be altered by the most random circumstance, symmetry and order reduced to a dull pattern by the display of an alternative, after which hard work will be needed to put the original values back in place.

In the flat a slight disturbance in the atmosphere, a vase moved from its place, alerted me to the fact that Rob had made one of his unscheduled visits. He obviously considered himself entitled to do this, even considered it to be a place that was rightfully his. He was justified in so doing by virtue of the fact that he had contributed to its upkeep over the years. It was entirely possible that he might want to move in, to take over, in which case I should have to find a flat of my own. This might be preferable in any case; it could be presented as a fait accompli, and moreover could be attributed to my disappointing character and history. I should give him my address, and our relations would henceforth be purely nominal. This, I saw, was the way to resolve our mutual antagonism. Leaving would be difficult; staying would be worse. I resolved to start looking as soon as possible. Once truly on my own I might have a greater sense of possibilities. The prospect was not pleasant, but the activity would be useful. And I need not fear dispossession, which, though not a real threat, would, I knew, make me restless if I did nothing to cancel it.

I had expected others to take care of my life. Now I saw how trusting and how profoundly wrong this had been. The trust could be put down to youth, and inexperience. And maybe there was no longer that limitless time in which those benevolent others would step forward and point the way. It was even possible that others might not have my best interests at heart, might prove as intent on their own destiny as I had thought to be on mine.

The message of most days, when scrutinized, was that nothing is as it seems, that events are unexpected, that people are surprising in ways one had not anticipated, and, most of all, that there are limits to one's knowledge. Philip Hudson was kind, a proud father, and a man whom melancholy had not rendered unsociable. Michael had not followed me, despite our closeness, and his image was fading even as I tried to recapture it. It had been a pleasant day, but the pleasure was low-key, unemotional. Then there had been that sighting of a truth that was not negotiable, a revelation from which I could take no comfort. When I went to lock the front door I saw a slip of paper in the letter box. I unfolded it. 'Emma,' said the tiny cautious handwriting. 'I came but you were not here. Sorry to miss you. Michael.'

11

A LETTER FROM FRANÇOISE BROUGHT NEWS OF A SORT: I could no longer write to her flat in the Boulevard Diderot because it had been repossessed and she could not trust the landlord (in effect the repossessor) to forward her mail. For the moment she was at her mother's house, on holiday, but this situation could not continue. She wondered whether I intended to retain my hotel room, for which I paid by the month, or whether she might use it until she found an alternative. Perhaps, if I were coming to Paris, she could meet me and discuss this. Also, she added, almost as an afterthought, could I keep the last weekend in September free? Her mother was giving a small lunch party, and they would both like me to be present.

This letter struck me as odd for several reasons. It heralded a redistribution of living space with which I had barely come to terms on my own account, almost forcing me to decide whether or not to return to Paris. I did not see why Françoise should not make her own arrangements, until I remembered how fatalistic she was in some respects, always preferring the quick and easy solution. This had been the case in the Boulevard Diderot: the flat had been borrowed from a departing friend, and she had simply stayed on until the friend stopped paying the rent. She may or may not have had the money to put this haphazard arrangement on to a proper basis; this was always a difficult matter to discuss. Clearly my hotel room would present the same rent-free advantages, particularly if I took my time in coming to a decision. And to be fair I had given no sign of forward planning, although she knew that I should have to collect my remaining possessions at some point. My immediate priority was to find a flat in London, but I had not entirely renounced my hotel room, keeping it as a useful pied-à-terre, at least for the foreseeable future, until I had checked all my references and had more or less finished my work.

As the Ancients knew, luxury weakens both the body and the resolve. The flat in which I had grown up, and which I knew so well, was by no means luxurious but its comforts were insidious and in any case habitual; I took for granted the fact that everything was in place and that if I moved out I should have to start again from nothing. At the same time there was the threat of a permanent invasion from Rob, in comparison with which bare floorboards and uncurtained windows would be a small price to pay. My room in Paris was after all only a temporary expedient. What had begun as a romantic adventure (but had never become one) was no longer invested with its original aura. By this reckoning there was no reason why Françoise should not move in, at least until she had decided what to do. I could not avoid the knowledge that I should be subsidizing her, any more than I could avoid the knowledge that she was obliging me to do something that she should be doing for herself, but this reasoning seemed so petty that I managed to discard it. Besides, I missed the sort of friend that Françoise had been to me, decisive, hospitable . . . I was by no means her equal. The fact that we did not fully understand one another was of little importance. I had much to learn from her, and indeed this was my opportunity to do so. We should have to share that room, for some remnant of common sense told me that it would be ungracious to prevaricate, and I should simply let her know if I would be needing it for an extended period.

Besides, I reminded myself, there were other hotel rooms, although that line of thought led back to Françoise, and what I knew of her other activities, and I let it go. I should write asking her how she was, how her mother was, and tell her how much I looked forward to that lunch party. A resolution would surely come about through the simple agency of our friendship. I reminded myself that it was time to abandon the sort of assumptions I had always made about characters and situations and become more pragmatic. In the end I wrote fondly to her, sending my best wishes to her mother, and said that I should be in Paris the following week and looked forward to seeing her at our usual café. Then I went out to post the letter before I changed my mind.

On my way to the bank to pick up more currency I passed a couple of estate agents, went in and registered my modest requirements, and was immediately presented with a list of what was available. I had not thought this would be easy: I had in mind a hopeless quest, as if I were applying for a visa. Instead there were photographs of palatial interiors, all desirable, all expensive, too expensive for me. My mother had left me a surprising amount of money, but this would have to last me until I found proper work, which might take some time. 'I really only want something quite small,' I apologized. The two girls who had been looking after me exchanged a glance. The one who had introduced herself as Alexandra said, 'Actually, I'm selling my flat.'

'She's getting married,' said the other one gleefully.

Alexandra raised her eyes to heaven. 'Jane, please. It's only one bedroom,' she said, 'but it's in a good area. I've been very happy there. Would you want to rent or buy?'

'Oh, buy,' I said firmly. 'As soon as possible.'

I could see it on Monday, she said. Not today, unfortunately; she was going straight down to the country after work, to stay with her fiancé's parents. Monday was cutting things fine; I had intended to leave for Paris, but another day or two would not hurt. And I should feel easier in my mind if I had made at least one decision, and such a vital one. Strangely enough I felt confident that this one flat, which I might not have time to properly examine, would provide the answer to my problem.

'Are you leaving any furniture?' I heard myself asking.

Another quick glance was exchanged with the other girl. 'That could be arranged. If you'd like to call in on Monday?'

'Monday morning?'

'Not before eleven, if that's okay.'

'I'll see you on Monday, then. I thought I'd have to wait weeks.'

'It's because everyone's away. We're usually frightfully busy.'

They were nice girls, rather like nurses, and about my age, twenty-six or twenty-seven. I looked respectfully at their desks, their names displayed on small plaques, at their computers and telephones. Not only did I want Alexandra's flat, I wanted her share of this office, and the exuberant company of her friend and colleague. No harm could come to me in such an environment. My other arrangements suddenly seemed almost illusory, fictitious, fabricated in a different context at a different time, too ambitious, too difficult for one of my cautious temperament. I was ready, indeed anxious, to retreat to the safe haven of modest conformity, and to leave French gardens where they belonged, their mute elegance in no need of my intervention. Those gardens now appeared hermetic, mysterious, not willing to divulge their secrets to the merely earnest. I wanted to be like those girls, or to have friends like those girls, uncritical, undemanding, undamaged by the scepticism that animates the French. To get married, like Alexandra, suddenly seemed to me highly desirable. The protection I had always longed for—that most people long for—would, if I managed to abandon a way of life I now saw as false, be within my grasp. At the same time I knew it was a matter of honour to complete what I had started and to accept the difficulties inherent in that task. Those difficulties encompassed Françoise and her demands, the absent Michael, and Rob, who would undoubtedly blame me for this further show of independence, an independence which might become ever more burdensome. I determined to take the flat, even sight unseen. In the absence of any other sign of protection it would have to do.

I passed the weekend in a fever of speculation, almost desperate to make the time pass, and was at the estate agent's well before eleven o'clock on Monday morning. 'She's not here yet,' said Jane, whom I thought of as the other girl. 'Would you like a coffee?' Through the windows, between the photographs of all those desirable properties, the sun shone hot and brilliant. 'She's very lucky,' said Jane. 'She's marrying a client. She met him here. *And* she sold him a house, exactly the one she wanted to live in. If that's not salesmanship I don't know what is. Ah, here's her car. Don't you want your coffee?'

'Actually, I'm rather anxious to get on,' I said. 'I'll no doubt be back later.'

'Good weekend?' I enquired of Alexandra, since that appeared to strike the right casual note. I longed to question her not only about the flat but about her way of life. I knew it was a mistake to let my eagerness show, that my approach was all wrong, that my growing restlessness might falsify the entire transaction, that she might be, almost certainly would be, used to a different sort of client. 'I have to go back to France next week, or rather this week,' I explained. 'That's why I seem in rather a hurry.'

'That's okay,' she said. 'We're here.'

'Here' was a small street off the King's Road: Jubilee Place. I liked the name, which seemed quirky and endearing, rather like *Coronation Street,* a programme my mother and I watched with grave attention, thinking it contained pointers to modern life. The flat, on the first floor, looked out on to the windows of the opposite building; it was small and undistinguished, but no more so than my hotel room. What furniture there was—a bed, two armchairs, and a large dining table which had clearly come from parental stock—was shabby. On a small shelf in the bedroom stood a row of children's classics: *Black Beauty, Little Women, The Secret Garden.* She saw me looking at them and smiled. 'I read them all the time,' she said. As I should. 'Will you leave them?' I asked.

'I suppose so. I'll have to grow up now, shan't I? You like it, then?'

'I love it. How much do you want for it?'

She named a sum I thought astronomical and which I automatically accepted. I should have liked to take possession immediately, but that was not possible. She could give me a month, she said. She was now, I saw, reluctant to hand it over, but my offer was too good to turn down. When I saw her begin to waver I reached into my bag for my chequebook and wrote her a cheque for the full amount.

'You *are* in a hurry,' she said, disconcerted.

'Well, as I explained, I have to go to France at the end of the week.' I felt suddenly exhausted.

'What exactly do you do?'

But I was not going to get into that. 'When can I have the keys?'

'If you'd like to call into the office when you come back . . . ,' she said. 'When will that be?'

'I don't know exactly. Not long.'

'Right,' she said, slightly crestfallen now at the prospect. She was more used to the hard sell, less adept at dealing with this sort of pressure. I felt briefly as though I had the upper hand.

'Would you like some coffee?' I asked, less anxious now to have her as a friend.

'I'd better get back,' she said. 'You're sure about this?'

'Oh, yes. Quite sure.'

'Emma Roberts,' she said thoughtfully, looking yet again at the cheque.

'It's quite all right,' I told her. 'It won't bounce.'

This was so crude that I blushed. 'Do forgive me. I'm not used to this. And do call me Emma.'

In the street I was struck by the noise, the activity. It was like waking from a dream, and like waking left me slightly dazed. I thought I should eat something, or at least drink some coffee, and sat down at a café table and ordered a sandwich. This was now my territory, but I could not spare it much attention. What I had to do was make my ownership public, or as public as was possible. What did one do in these circumstances? One wrote letters, one went to the bank, the post office. Instead I got into a taxi and went back to what I now thought of as my mother's flat, and sat at the kitchen table, perplexed. I should have liked to sleep, but knew that this would be dangerous. I had, for the time being at least, to put matters in train, so that I could consider the episode closed. There was the matter of the hotel room to be decided. I was now of a mind to pay the rent until the end of the year, as a precaution. It was obvious that Françoise might prove a problem, but I was now safe—or safer—in the certainty that I had a home of my own. My residual uneasiness, I found, had slightly diminished, but had not altogether vanished.

I sat down at my mother's desk and prepared to write my

letters. This was a mistake. In the drawer I saw her pen, her cards, her small packet of tissues. I thought that I could smell her scent, but this was mere illusion. She came most vividly to mind when I knew that I should take nothing away from here. I wanted it to remain hers and now saw the rightness of handing it over to Rob. One day I might come back, might even be glad to do so. But I sensed that that day was a long way off, at the end of my life, perhaps, and could not—should not—be anticipated.

'Dear Rob,' I wrote. 'You will not be too surprised to hear that I have bought a small flat and shall be moving into it at the end of the month.' (Here I gave him the address and the telephone number, which I had memorized.) 'I find I cannot stay here; my mother's clothes are still in the wardrobe, her brushes on her dressing table. Perhaps this is why I sleep so badly. I shall be dividing my time between London and Paris, where I still have work to do, and of course will keep in touch. The purpose of this letter is to ask you to move in here, to take possession of a place you know so well, and to which you have as much right as I have. I know you have always thought of it as your proper home: why else would you have kept the keys? This situation has worried me and I should feel easier in my mind knowing where I can reach you at any time. Eventually, I suppose, the flat will revert to me, but that day seems a long way off. I dare say you will disapprove, as you always have done, but on reflection will see this as a sensible move. I shall get in touch as soon as I have settled in. I hope you will be comfortable here. As I say, you will know where to reach me if you want to or need to. Yours, Emma.' I could not think of a more affectionate way of signing off, and this seemed to me a sorry state of affairs. But it was too late to enter into more intimate terms with this strange relic of a family that was no longer a family, and I left it.

Quite suddenly my previous exhilaration left me, and I sat stunned by the fact that I had so easily removed myself from what I had always known. If I clung to anyone or anything it was to the girl Alexandra and her equanimity in a similar situation. But then her future was clearly mapped out, whereas mine was a succession of empty days. Sheer displacement activity would be needed to keep me going, and I could see myself inventing further tasks in order to furnish my life with meaning. I could, for instance, start looking for the sort of things one needed in a new home; instead I sat almost motionless, in an access of dread. It was almost the end of the afternoon before I could rouse myself, and then my first instinct was to go out and walk the streets of my childhood, as if I should never see them again.

As always, walking proved therapeutic, but the relief was only momentary. Back in the flat I wrote more letters: it was important to me that people should know where I was. I wrote again to Françoise, giving her the details and the new telephone number, but telling her that I should see her in Paris before the move took place. She would not be too interested in my movements in London; only those in Paris were of relevance to her. And I knew that she had preoccupations of her own, of which I had had a brief glimpse. It was even possible that she shared my longing for a settled future, though not the one for which her mother destined her. In comparison, Alexandra's happy, open face struck me as phenomenal. If I wanted anything it was a chance to know something of that ease. I wrote to Michael at the hotel, telling him how sad I was to have missed him, told him that I should be in Paris in the next few days, and that I hoped we could see each other. I had a sense of finality here, as if a great deal of time had elapsed since our last meeting. I wrote to Sarah Cartwright, who had kindly thought to provide me with a partner. And then, greatly daring, I wrote to Philip Hudson, who had also been kind, perhaps more than kind. 'You mentioned that you sometimes walked home from your hospital in Chelsea,' I wrote. 'I am moving shortly to a flat in Jubilee Place: this is my new telephone number. I should like it so much if you would come and have a drink one evening. We could resume our discussion, which I remember as fruitful. I sincerely hope that you will get in touch. Yours ever, Emma Roberts.'

12

I ARRIVED IN PARIS TO FIND SEVERAL OF FRANÇOISE'S effects liberally scattered over my room. This disconcerted me: the dull conformity I was used to precluded such speed, such alacrity. I could just understand her need to escape her mother's formidable will, but I had not foreseen that it would be replicated so faithfully.

In the wider scheme of things none of this was overwhelmingly important. But one is territorial by nature, and the smell of Françoise's scent overriding what was left of my own was difficult to tolerate. I wondered how to extract us both from this situation, for I felt the onus was on me to do so. Surely friendship was more significant than possession? Perhaps this is true in an ideal world, but I could not easily dismiss the dismay that was my initial reaction on seeing those familiar black garments flung hastily onto the bed, shoes kicked off in the middle of the room, and an alien hairbrush on the bedside table. Yet I knew that coming to terms with this disorder was the price I would have to pay for any kind of peace. Instinctively I resisted change: I was more affected than I had realized by my impulsive purchase of the flat, although it had seemed reasonable enough at the time. Various sensible solutions presented themselves and were dismissed. It seemed that I had no recourse but to accept what others had decided. I thought with a wince of the sound of Rob's keys in the door, in comparison with which this dilemma was derisory. Yet there would have to be a discussion in which I should have to lay down certain rules, and here I knew I should be at a disadvantage. It was Françoise, the stronger character, who made the rules, and who was effortlessly, permanently indulgent to what she thought of as my slightly backward desire to behave well, or at least according to the original instructions.

I went to the desk, and already I could feel the pleading smile spreading across my face. Mme Denise, the owner's sister, was not delighted to see me. I explained, redundantly, that my friend would be occupying the room until I reclaimed it. When would that be, she demanded. All this was irregular. I pointed out that the room was paid for until September, two months ahead, and in a moment of weakness said that I should like to retain it until the end of the year. At the sight of the cheque she was slightly mollified, but we both knew that I had lost face, that the transaction was wholly to the advantage of others. In the short term, I said cheerfully, I should need another room. It seemed that there were no other rooms, *les va-*

cances being offered as an explanation. I had already noticed the unfamiliar presence of predominantly young tourists, many with rucksacks, some with guidebooks, unaware that their presence was barely tolerated when the maids wanted to clean as quickly as possible and to leave while they could still enjoy a few hours of sunshine. The glorious weather was another factor that could not be ignored: I too wanted to be out. It was my sudden access of impatience that won the day; I could even feel a rising tide of annoyance, which must have been reflected in my expression. There is a small room, she said reluctantly, on the top floor. It was the room she normally kept for her son when he wanted to spend a few days, or rather nights, in Paris. She was expecting him at the end of the week, and could therefore let me have it only for a few days. She named a price that was clearly improvised. That will do very well, I said, but when I returned in September I expected to find Mlle Desnoyers in another room, if necessary the one I was now expected to occupy. At this she favoured me with a rare smile. *'On s'était habitué à vous,'* she said. This accolade—that my presence was tolerated, even appreciated—did something to ease my sense of unfamiliarity. Also I was anxious to get out into the air, to walk, to drink in the sun. There was nothing I could do until the evening, when presumably Françoise would be in evidence. Of Michael I did not allow myself to think. I knew, without having been told, that he was not in Paris, a fact confirmed by Mme Denise, *les vacances* again being offered by way

131

of explanation. When was he expected to return, I asked. She shrugged. That she could not tell me. But I could, if I wished, leave a note.

The room to which I was directed was very small and very hot. There was a faint smell of cigarettes, which indicated that the son had used it fairly recently. Most of the space was taken up by the bed; the window looked down into a well from which rose the voices of the hotel servants. There was no possibility of remaining there during the hours of daylight; even nighttime would be curtailed, for one would only return there to snatch a few hours' sleep. The absence of a view depressed me, and I regretted the friendly windows of Jubilee Place, even more so the green vistas seen from my mother's flat. Strangely I no longer thought of that flat as home. Indeed I could not attach the concept of home to any of the places I was now obliged to occupy. All appeared random, even makeshift. This seemed to be my fate: to live in ever-smaller rooms at an age when I should have been expanding into wider territory. Yet I had spent, or forfeited, so much money that I was forced to accept this. An argument erupted in the courtyard far below me, and I left the room determined to force someone to recognize my rights, though sadly aware that such a person did not exist.

But away from the room, outside in the street, I found the world still beautiful. Since I had nothing to do until the evening I took the route all tourists take, into the centre of town, where

I should be at one with all the Americans on their regular pilgrimage. I felt like a tourist, a visitor, no longer entitled to claim even a momentary citizenship. I sat for half an hour in the Tuileries, watching the children sail their boats, then I crossed the bridge, walked up the rue de Seine to the Place Saint-Sulpice, where I drank too many cups of coffee. My footsteps led me to the rue de l'Odéon, the Boulevard Saint-Germain, to the rue des Saints Pères. . . . When I was tired I went back to the Place Saint-Sulpice, but this time sat in the vast church, where a scattering of devout women and a silent sacristan were my companions. Their presence reminded me that not all is calculation and false assurances, that somehow it is possible to cling to belief, to proceed in good faith, to cherish the alliances that one has made in earlier life, and above all to feel fortified by one's observances. This, unfortunately, was not possible for me: I was alone, and most memories were troubled, but I took a certain comfort from being with those women, none of them smart or confident, but serious in a way I could appreciate. It was the seriousness, the silence, far removed from the glitter of the sun, the voices of passersby, the sheer activity of the outside world, that spoke to me. There were perhaps no more than six or seven women in the huge church, each immured in her own thoughts, none giving obvious signs of devotion, but dignified in their isolation. This again was not something to which I could lay claim; my own inheritance was without lustre, an affair of fractured alliances, put together in an uncomplaining, even peaceful way, but a way that bequeathed little in the way of certainty. I felt that mine was an improvised life, doomed to further improvisations, and that any certainties would have to be borrowed from others. Feeling a little fraudulent I lit a candle. Again conformity beckoned, but I had been cursed with independence (which I now saw quite clearly as something of a burden). I must make my way unaided. I smiled at one of the women as we left the church together. She glanced at me, incurious. Her expression told me, more eloquently than any words, that I was not in any way like her, that she had no need of my kind, and that she had placed me as a foreigner, a further step in the process of alienation that had dogged me since I had arrived earlier in the day.

It was too early to eat, so I sat in the Place and drank more coffee. This was one of the longest days I could remember, the longest and the most inconsequential. There was little comfort to be had from the knowledge that it would soon be over. Faces now expressed tiredness, but also satisfaction that the pilgrimage had done its work. It would be light until nine, or even slightly later, but there was an intimation of the evening to come, a slowing down of pace; even a diminution of noise. The coffee I had drunk all through the day had made me nervous, even a little angry, but I knew that what was needed was an assumption of equanimity, and with that equanimity a determination—quiet, understated if possible—to resolve matters in my favour. None of it really mattered, but I was tired, longing for a bath, longing even to be back in London. The softness of the evening was not for me, try as I might to claim part of it as my own.

The sound of running taps proclaimed Françoise's presence; she was in a sense taking the bath I longed for. I knocked and went in. Françoise emerged from the bathroom drying her hair.

'Emma! *Quel bon vent . . . ?*'

Her surprise was completely genuine. She embraced me fondly, then sat on the bed, still towelling her hair.

'Why didn't you tell me you were coming?' she asked.

'Didn't you get my letter? Or rather letters?'

She looked puzzled. 'About your mother? Of course I did. But we've seen each other since then, Emma. You came down. Don't you remember?'

'I mean my most recent letter, saying I was coming back.'

'I can't remember. When was this?'

It seemed too clumsy to spell out the times and dates of my letters. In any event it was clear that she had forgotten all about me.

'I need the room, Françoise. It is mine, after all. And it's paid for. I can't afford . . .'

'But, Emma, you said I could borrow it when you weren't here.'

'I'm here now.' I sounded peevish, obstinate.

'And I'm late for dinner. Can we discuss this later? Or, better still, tomorrow morning? How long are you staying?'

I had intended to spend at least a week in Paris, possibly longer. But now it seemed that I had little choice but to leave. Again I was aware that I was wasting both time and money.

'How do I look?' she asked, posing for my benefit. She was wearing her usual black trousers, and a black sweater with a deep neckline that revealed a stretch of taut tanned skin. She looked perfectly adapted to the Parisian evening, and in addition excited, as I had never seen her before. Her dark good looks, too emphatic for mere prettiness, too sardonic for beauty, had gained a new patina. Initially, before I had got to know her, I had been slightly intimidated by the black brows, the strong mouth, the powerful nose; now I saw all these features as winning cards in an ancient game, the game one plays by stealth, and by whatever means one can command. One would not willingly cross Françoise, or even engage her in an argument. That was why and how I had always been uncritical in her company. And now she seemed to have grown in assurance, in authority, as if she had right on her side. With sinking heart I realized that she had won the argument, without the argument even having taken place.

'You remember the café?' she was saying. 'The café where we sometimes met for coffee? When you were working in the library.'

'Of course I remember it,' I said. 'I haven't been away that long.'

'It seems ages. Why don't we meet there tomorrow morning? Not too early, though. You're not in a hurry, are you?'

'I'll be there at ten,' I said.

A hand went up to her forehead in a pretty gesture. 'But that is early, Emma. Make it eleven. I've got so much to tell you. When are you leaving?'

I had not said I was leaving. She had decided for me.

'Until tomorrow, then,' I said, turning to go.

'Wait a minute. You've got dust all over your jacket. Here, let me brush it for you.' The brush—my brush—was wielded vigorously. 'There,' she said. 'That's better.' She gave me one of her old critical looks. 'You look tired. Are you all right?'

I felt, in fact, rather faint, and reminded myself that I had eaten very little that day. 'I'm fine. Have a good evening.' It seemed necessary to leave, and I was suddenly anxious to be on my own, even if it meant sitting in that other room, the room of my exile. I could feel my feet dragging as I made my way to the lift. There were different voices to be heard, different scents permeating the corridors. All around me preparations were being made, but I no longer cared. I would go out for a meal and then simply have an early night. I knew that in my case early nights were associated with sorrow, that the mere fact of closing one's eyes could bring a feeling of dread, but by now I was too tired to care. It was important to husband my strength for the argument that would have to take place on the following day. And yet argument was too strong a word for the friendly discussion, in which it was important not to show anger, not to express surprise, not, in fact, to proclaim and exert one's rights . . . Once again it seemed perverse, and more than that, uncouth, to refer to matters of ownership, to arrangements which had not been honoured. For what was clear was that Françoise had no intention of giving up the room, and that it was up to me to negotiate my way out of this difficulty with the best grace I could muster.

I slept so deeply that when I woke it seemed as though a decade had passed and I could view the whole episode with detachment. I was possessed of several unalterable truths, the chief of which was that it is useless to argue with those who are cleverer than oneself, in whom superior strategies are already in place. I also—and this was welcome—saw the beauty of work, of the sort of work I did, in which evidence is sought and verification called for. I was destined by nature to follow that path, and by the same token to do rather less well in the business of real life, for to perceive and point out inconsistencies was, to use Mme Desnoyers's classification, *mal élevé*. The first part of my adventure was thus over, and if I were the loser in one sense it might be that the desire for truth was always inconvenient. Françoise would both gain and lose by this; the friendship, maintained on the surface, would be flawed from within. The saving grace was that there need be no call for explanations: in that way a sort of victory had been achieved on both sides. I should, of course, let her have her way. There remained the problem of her mother's lunch party, which it would be ungracious not to attend. But that could be decided at a later date.

I got up, dressed, picked up my bag, and went downstairs. It was early, too early to make practical decisions. Another perfect day was on offer, and with the streets still quiet I was in a position to make the best of it. I thought of my flat, as one might think of an alibi, and told myself that that at least was not disputed territory. This reasoning was not entirely satisfactory, but in the interests of truth I should have to accommodate it. And I could be back there this evening, for there was clearly no point in remaining in Paris. The work I had still to do could be undertaken without preliminary warnings of my presence. I could even find another hotel. Unfortunately some of my possessions remained in my old room, and arrangements would have to be made if I were not to forfeit those as well.

I sat down, much too early, at our original table in the corner of the café, from which I could monitor comings and goings, the life of the street, as I loved to do. Françoise would be late: that too I had foreseen. But in this new mood of enlightenment I saw that this was irrelevant, and in any case the beauty of the day was compensation enough. It was just past eleven-thirty when she arrived, looking harassed, but also vivacious, as if she too had arrived at a certain code of behaviour,

whether or not it was entirely convincing. Yet it was with genuine pleasure that we contemplated each other, as if for a few
moments at least, our original friendship had suffered no incursions.

'You had a good evening?' I enquired.

'Marvellous.' Her expression cleared. Now she was telling
the truth. That was the truth on which part of my mind had
alighted: sex.

'Someone new?'

'Someone new.'

Clearly this was classified information. I was wryly amused.
Not only had the room been repossessed; it had been repossessed for a specific purpose.

'And your mother?'

'Naturally, my mother is outside of all this. She has to be.'

'And her plans are still intact?'

She looked troubled. Her mother was the one factor she
was unable to dispose of.

I did not ask what those plans were. She had always been
adept at improvisation, whereas her mother was the complete
opposite. They were alike only in their obduracy.

'My mother talks of living in Paris again. She was born
here, you know. She thinks it would be good to return. She is
still quite young, fifty-nine, and she would like to go out more.
It is not good for her to be stuck in the country. Not fair,
really.'

'But the house?'

'That will come to me, of course.'

If she married that man in the tight blazer, if he and his fearful mother, in exchange for money, were allowed to take over, if the two adversaries could agree on the price of a flat in Paris, if Françoise could agree to live under the surveillance of a mother-in-law as exacting as her own mother: these were imponderables which it would be unkind to disturb.

'I look forward to your mother's party,' I said. 'Incidentally, I shall need my room for that weekend. If you don't mind.'

'Of course. I shall probably be at home, helping out.' She sighed.

'And is this to announce your engagement?'

'No!' That was instinctive. But we both knew that that was understood.

'What will you do today?' I asked, anxious to spare her discomfort.

'I shall see my friend again. We are meeting for lunch.' She looked at her watch, then at mine, to check the time. 'I mustn't be late. I'm sorry we have so little time together. Perhaps if you come back ... Well, of course you will. What time do you leave?'

'I can take the next train out. I should be home by this evening.'

I noticed that I had referred to the flat as home, quite naturally. This was an advance. And I had better set about making it entirely habitable. When the darker days and longer nights set in I might even be glad to be there.

We both stood up to leave. 'My friend is American,' she said, with a smile that was the nearest thing to transparency that I had ever perceived in her. She was in love, that much was clear. I smiled back. We embraced with genuine affection. I stood for a moment and watched her retreating figure. When she reached the corner she looked back and raised her hand. It was as if some tie united her to me, to earlier days before friendship became blurred. My feeling was one of relief that I had said and done nothing to alter the behaviour we had agreed upon.

I picked up my bag and walked to the Métro. As if by a law stronger than chance a train was waiting for me at the Gare du Nord. As I had foreseen—but without calculation—I should be home by evening.

13

'I HAVE A MORAL PROBLEM,' I SAID TO PHILIP HUDSON, after placing a glass of wine on a small table beside his chair.

'Oh, dear.'

'I want to know how far one should indulge one's friends.'

'We're urged to go the extra mile. Or so says some American president or other, cribbing from the gospels, as ever: go with him twain. One tries to be sympathetic, of course. I don't know about indulgence. A male friend?'

'No, a woman. One with a very strong will.'

'If she has a very strong will she is in no need of your indulgence.'

'I suppose not. I may have to get used to this idea. Would you like a smoked salmon sandwich?'

'I should, yes.'

'Are you eating out tonight?'

'No. A couple of sandwiches will be fine. I'll look in at the hospital, to see a patient.'

This was his second visit to me in three weeks and already it seemed entirely natural. I had a wistful desire for company which was alleviated, partly, by his presence. By now attuned to his opportunistic eating habits, I found it agreeable to do some respectable shopping so that I could always offer him something. I did not go so far as to provide the makings of a meal, but smoked fish, cheeses, fruit in season could be produced without effort and would not betray undue thought on my part. Indeed the very point of the foresight was the shopping itself. I had found it depressing to accumulate additions to the flat, simply on my own behalf, although I now had the money to do so. A letter from Rob, expressing an exasperation with me that was all too familiar, contained the news that my mother's income from investments would now come to me, and that if I needed any advice I could reach him at the flat. This I had no intention of doing, but the money enabled me to buy a new bed, new linen, a small table, and some cups and plates, on one of which I now arranged several smoked salmon sandwiches and an apple.

I was happy to do this, indeed more than happy, not because I felt it natural to do so, but because the experience of providing for myself alone contained a faint foreknowledge of what it would be like to grow old in this way. The settled circumstances into which I had retreated would, I knew, begin to irk me with their suggestion of permanence, unalterability. I missed the freedom of the hotel, the proximity of the busy street, the random nature of temporary living, which was in so many ways like a holiday. Even Françoise's incursions began to seem charmingly bohemian as I looked back on them from my rather dark flat, although no one here could displace or dispossess me. This acquisition of property made me feel older, or, rather, old. Every towel, every saucepan seemed to act as witness to my solitary condition, and this was paradoxical since I had always accepted this condition as perfectly normal, even sensible. It was a parody of a new life, one for which I had no profound need. I even took against my new possessions; the very plate I was holding was exonerated only by virtue of the fact that it contained food for someone other than myself. I was almost in a hurry to hand it over, to see another's appetite in action, and thereby free myself from the tyranny of my own arrangements. I did not question this. Whether it were a need for company or something more complicated, I welcomed the opportunity to act on another's behalf. And yet I knew and accepted that the life I had chosen was the only one I could manage, and though I looked towards a future which contained nothing more sinister than boredom I was also quite clear about its safety, however anodyne and irritating that might turn out to be.

'You're not nervous, living here alone?' he asked. 'Ah, delicious. Thank you.'

'Nervous? I have never been nervous. But restless, certainly. I think it's not natural to live alone. I go out as much as I can. Oh, I don't mean that I go to parties, entertainments of that kind. I mean I leave the flat in the morning as if I were going to work. That's what I really like, feeling at one with all the people who are really going to work, even if I'm only going to a reference library. Then I almost automatically leave at the same time as the other workers, the real ones. And I prefer to eat out, although I've got a perfectly good kitchen. Nothing elaborate. Sitting in a café suits me better than sitting at home. Would you like coffee?'

'Perhaps another glass of that wine.'

I was longing to ask him how he managed, whether his heart had been broken by his wife's defection, whether he longed for company, but had the sense to restrain myself. It would be impertinent for a woman of my age to put such questions to someone so much older—but how old was he? I had thought him to be in his fifties, but now I saw that this was an impression conveyed by his heavy build and his frequent silences. I revised it downwards to his late forties. The fact that he behaved like a man from whom youth has fled without leaving a vestige behind was neither here nor there. Youth had not done me much good either. And yet my longings were those of an adolescent: to be taken care of, to be nurtured, to be loved. All this I managed to conceal, as one should. It is an error to confess such needs. Nor is it entirely beneficial to perceive the existence of such needs in others. Needs are too personal, too intimate, and the fact that they may be shared does little to dignify them. So that Philip Hudson's needs, and indeed my own, remained safely out of sight.

'How long will you stay at the hospital?' I asked.

'Not more than half an hour.'

'And then will you walk back to York Street?'

'I expect so. Unless you'd like me to come back here?'

I must have blushed. With confusion, but also with pleasure. 'Another time,' I managed to say. 'I mean that.'

He smiled. 'At least that's settled. What will you do for the rest of the evening?'

'I don't know. Read, sit in a café. Or read *and* sit in a café. Actually I think I might walk a bit. Oh, don't worry. I'll leave you at the hospital. I think I'm rather homesick. And yet I am home; how strange. Perhaps it's a feeling that can descend on one at any time.'

'You think too much. Health is what matters, freedom from disease.'

'I'm sure you're right. Is that why you went into medicine?'

'I had a sister of whom I was very fond. She died young. I may have thought I could have helped her if I'd known rather more. Anyway I enjoy what I do.'

I knew that that was as much as I should get in the way of a shared confidence. His life could hardly have been immune from soul-searching, but this was not a process to which I had access. I rather liked his taciturnity. It was what I had liked about Michael.

'And your young man?' he asked, echoing my thoughts.

'He was not in Paris, where I expected to find him. I dare say we'll make contact sooner or later. I'll have to go back in any case. I left my raincoat there, a pair of shoes, that sort of thing. At the end of September, probably. I have an invitation I can't get out of.'

My homesickness may have been for a way of life that was no longer sustainable. I was now condemned to adulthood: nothing could have prevented that from happening. Anything less would be an evasion of responsibility. And yet those graceful unemployable students I had met in Paris, so poetic in their artist's garb, so accessible in their liberal attitude to time and place, had seemed entirely viable: no trace of homesickness there. But of course they were home; they were part of the culture, the last gasp of the Romantic Movement. And they were loved for their emblematic status. I had seen many a noncommittal café owner pour one or other of them—it hardly mattered which—a free glass of wine. They paid with their charm, which was entirely genuine; in return they were cherished for their unspoiled aspirations. They also had the saving grace of knowing their role, of shouldering their inheritance, and if in time they acquired a certain cynicism they managed to make that equally attractive.

The difference between these archetypes and this man now walking beside me could not have been greater: it was the difference between a tenor and a bass. My present companion was responsible, respectable, a man of substance, not only physically but emotionally as well: grown-up. Part of his gravitas derived from his consistency, and yet part of me longed for the emotional range, however superficial, of that other species, and of those I had left behind, together with my own eagerness, my own spontaneity. If I were to please now I should have to be circumspect, as he was. I wondered if I had said too much, been too introspective. This was not the mode in this country to which I had returned and where I was now in exile. Perhaps there was a balance to be struck between the two. Perhaps what I really wanted was my old room back, but this line of thinking led to Françoise, and I was no longer sure that I wanted to attend her mother's lunch party. Getting out of it, however, might prove difficult, since I had been invited some weeks in advance. But I had over a month in which to work this out, and the evening was too fine to be spoiled with such considerations, and I could spare little attention for this matter, although it would, in time, acquire a certain urgency.

The evening was indeed so beautiful that mere conversation seemed otiose. Even very young people, intent on their own activities, drifted, idled, as if nostalgic for the summer that was already on the wane. It was late July, a poignant moment in the year's evolution. The sky was already darkening, although the light had nothing about it that was threatening. But everyone seemed possessed of the knowledge that high summer would only return after an achingly long interval, and regret was in the air. I found myself invaded by the strange concern that gripped me every night as I awaited the onset of sleep, in comparison with which waking was a relief. It was eight o'clock, too early to say goodbye to the day. Even this walk had something valedictory about it. Yet there was a crowd outside the cinema, waiting for the evening to renew itself; restaurants were embarking on their busiest time. Philip Hudson, perhaps succumbing to one of his periodic trances, said nothing, which seemed appropriate. I did not look forward to returning to the flat, to see the empty wine glass, the crumb-strewn plate, evidence of his departure. There was no sentiment in this, though perhaps something more subtle, an apprehension of a solitude that was no longer appropriate.

'You didn't eat your apple,' I said. It was a beautiful apple, though I did not know its name. I could imagine its texture as a corrective to the salmon.

'It's in my pocket. I'll eat it later.'

We stopped and faced each other. 'Don't linger,' he said. 'Thank you for a pleasant evening.'

I held out my hand. 'I shall probably stay here until September. And you? Will you go away?'

'No. I don't take holidays.'

'You said you had a house in Winchelsea. . . .'

'It's rented out. I hardly use it. Mark was fond of it when he was young. He rarely goes there now.'

'What a shame.' This sounded falsely polite. 'Good night, then.' I turned away, feeling a little uncomfortable. I did not look back.

The question of Paris seemed hardly to arise. It was now quite clear to me that what I had fashioned into a simulacrum of a home had been taken over and that I had no choice but to accept my flat as a form of permanence for which I had no taste. That this was perfectly irrational did nothing to allay my fears. Theoretically I was free to come and go as I pleased, to alight in one temporary refuge after another, if that was what I really wanted. And it seemed as though that was what I really did want: it was permanence that frightened me. I could and did appreciate that shifting and shiftless population to which I had become accustomed, and perhaps preferred it to any other. The troubadour inheritance brought with it a grace that was evident even in destitution. The best of those wandering scholars would turn into the very real scholars whose grey heads, bent over their work, I had observed morning after morning in the library. It had been there that Françoise, the earth mother, had functioned as an alternative mythology, which they now honoured from a certain distance. It was in that role that she flourished, was at her best. Divorced of her iconic status she was simply another woman, whose tastes and activities allied her with the real world, and whose power games with her mother belonged to a lesser mythology, to fiction, the sort of fiction for which the French are renowned. Better, I thought, to remain in one's most becoming manifestation than to enter into lesser forms of competition, of possession. What did it matter if the house changed hands? It was the house that would outlive its inhabitants, whose quarrels would be forgotten as soon as they had gone, leaving the light of changing seasons to illuminate its façade, perhaps for the benefit of other visitors delighted to have it in their sights.

And yet characters like Françoise are life-giving: they broaden one's outlook. Even their stratagems and deceits are instructive; one can observe them, marvel at them, even as one disapproves. I could imagine how she would have conducted the evening that had just passed: bold questions, a little mockery, an expectation that money would be spent, a predictable conclusion. She would have formed a more or less accurate assessment of his social position, his income, and treated him accordingly, perhaps in a way that most men would understand. I knew nothing about him beyond what he had told me, or was willing to tell me, choosing to remain discreet about what he was determined to conceal. In comparison I had talked too much, and at the same time said nothing of interest. This was not a useful way to proceed.

It had grown dark without my becoming aware of it and the streets were quieter now. I turned back towards the flat, though I had no desire to be there. Its emptiness, its silence had

once appealed to me; the fact that I was its undisputed owner
had been, but was no longer, persuasive. I wanted, almost all the
time, to be away from it, anxious to join others, if only symboli-
cally. My work benefited from this, but my assiduity had less to
do with my researches than with a desire to be significantly oc-
cupied, as if I were performing a task on someone else's behalf,
fictively, among the wage earners, or rather among those other
vague researchers, like myself. The company of the latter was
illusory: locked into our various obsessions we merely occu-
pied similar desks, exchanging few words, our heads bent at the
same angle. This was work that the normally constituted would
neither undertake nor understand. It was no wonder that I
made such a poor showing when in the company of others, still
less that I should admire, to the point of extravagance, characters of such decisive boldness that nothing that they ever did
could undermine my regard for them.

There were few lighted windows in Jubilee Place. It was
Friday, and many people had left for the weekend. I knew some
of these people by sight: we nodded pleasantly to each other,
but no more than that. The onset of the weekend was problematic in other ways: I could no longer take it for granted.
Those silent, or almost silent walks with Michael, in settings
which did not seek to impress, were not likely to be repeated:
we had almost certainly lost touch. Those suburban gardens
were in truth dearer to my heart than the grander counterparts
to which my attention was directed, yet part of the attraction

was the mild air of compatibility that united the strolling families, that peaceable kingdom. And maybe it had suited us both to be in that company. It would be difficult to convey this to anyone not of the same mind, most difficult of all to convince the self-sufficient, self-regarding characters I so admired.

The flat was dark and chilly, as it so often was. I did not immediately switch on lights or tidy the kitchen, but stood at the window, gazing out into the greater dark. Now it was possible to believe in autumn, even in winter. Tomorrow was Saturday; I should pretend to be domesticated. On Sunday I should walk, out of habit. A window across the street was suddenly, violently illuminated; if anything it emphasized the darkness. My bed in Paris had looked out on to a busy street. All night cars passed, footsteps sounded. I could hear voices in the hotel, taps running. Here I faced a small blank space between two unidentifiable buildings. The temporary euphoria of buying this flat had quite evaporated. In bed—expensive, comfortable—I waited with the usual trepidation for the onset of sleep. It was not wakefulness that disturbed me; it was sleep itself, that descent into the unfathomable, the unknown, the element that threatens us all. Here the silence seemed to possess its own threat. I regretted that Philip Hudson had not returned, as I had half hoped he would. A stealthy patter of rain, surprising after so fine an evening, would be my accompaniment through the dark hours. In the morning I would adjust my outlook to taking comfort where and when it was indicated.

14

THE NEXT FEW WEEKS WERE A HOT BLANK OF STIFLING days and steadily darkening evenings. With everyone away there seemed no incentive to work, to pursue my humble routine, and yet I progressed, settling down in the early morning to writing a page or two, before the superb light summoned me out of doors to fill the day as best I could. This I managed by returning to my task from time to time, so that the work—the book?—became my only activity. At the same time a certain caution inhibited me from too much assiduity, for this activity would have to see me through the winter and I knew that it would be unwise to anticipate an early conclusion. I had no authorial ambitions, but I did see that what I was doing was not entirely redundant: the work was on the whole honourable, if of no great interest to those who had not shared my experience of walking through those deserted gardens in inhospitable months, or searching for clues in old prints and ancient accounts, with only the sight of a decisive perimeter, of a harmonious crossing point, where two paths met in a conclusive right angle, to reawaken my belief in underlying principle—for that was the raison d'être of the whole undertaking.

I perceived the beauty of study itself, the process rather than the result, and once I put down my pen I felt regret, as though abandoning a friendship. The rest of the day seemed improvised, and it was sometimes difficult to find a reason to do anything else. The nights were even more of a problem, alleviated only by the occasional company of my unlikely friend, Philip Hudson. Neither of us talked much, as if by mutual consent, but his presence was easy to accept, based as it was on a decision to go no further than the occasion warranted. In this way an understanding was reached that seemed to suit us both, though this, again, was never openly discussed.

In fact my work was the only area of my life in which I could exercise my own will. This may be the reward for those who undertake such a solitary occupation. But if I felt that I possessed autonomy in this matter I was also aware that such autonomy generally failed me in the company of others, when I felt habitually at a loss. I envied Philip his straightforward occupation, as I saw it, and respected him for it, as must all those whose lives he saved. He probably regarded my work as the equivalent of embroidering a sampler, yet when I doggedly continued to amass my so far few pages he was rather kind, enjoining me not to tire my eyes, not to neglect proper exercise or meals. I was grateful for this, grateful too that no discussion of its merits would take place, and on the whole content with my life, which if not exactly interesting was not contentious or tiresome, and which was certainly as restful to me as it may have been to others.

This almost becalmed interlude was interrupted by a letter from Françoise reminding me of her mother's lunch party on the thirtieth. She had arranged for me to be driven down and back by a friend, M. de Robillard, who would collect me from the hotel at eleven-thirty and return me to Paris some time in the late afternoon or early evening. He would be with his daughter, Mme Mauvoisin, whom she was sure I would find sympathetic. She added that she was looking for a permanent flat in Paris—for the moment she was staying with her mother—and should be out of the hotel some time in the future. From this I deduced that I should have to find another room, and I was almost grateful to her for letting me know this in advance. She was so looking forward to seeing me, she said, and although there would be little opportunity to talk at the party we could arrange to meet once she had discharged her various duties. Her mother sent her best regards. Naturally she, Françoise, was anxious that the occasion should be a success, particularly as her mother had put a great deal of thought into it. She hoped that I would find it interesting. She herself could not wait for it to be over.

Like most of Françoise's exchanges this left a great deal unsaid. There was no word, for example, of the American lover, whose presence in Paris might or might not be her reason for staying in the same place. Equally there was no word of her feelings for him, though I had reason to believe that these were genuine. What did he do? Where did they meet? What were his feelings for her? Naturally I could not put these questions to her: she would only tell me if she felt inclined to do so. My role, as ever, was to be discreet. It was my discretion that commended me, as it may have done to her mother. I was destined to be a listener, not even an observer, one from whom no adverse comment, no untoward question could be expected. My very tact had a certain social value: I could be relied upon to be agreeable, to mingle without making a strong impression. Part of me was resigned to this; it was a role I knew well and could discharge automatically. Long silence had accustomed me to such behaviour, and allowed me to reach my own conclusions without undue prompting. And in any case I should be among strangers. On reflection it was kind of them to have invited me. And possibly there was some acknowledgement on Françoise's part that she was in a way—always vague, always unspecified— in my debt, quite literally so, as she was living at my expense. I now saw this as a perfectly natural arrangement. My presence at her mother's party was her way of discharging this debt. I admired the thinking behind this, and reminded myself that I must adjust my attitude to the convention that had brought this about.

I was tempted to write back with some excuse that I

could not leave London, but I knew that this would be regarded as a grave breach of protocol. And although my presence would not be missed, would not even be noticed, I was bound by the strength of previous arrangements to attend, and to send a suitably appreciative letter of thanks once I was home again. Besides, I could think of no excuse that would pass muster, and, if anything, shared a distaste for such stratagems as would certainly be evinced by Mme Desnoyers. I knew two things simultaneously: that I was unwilling to disturb my present routine, and that I was permanently unwilling to give offence. I was almost used to my quiet days and to the evenings when I could look forward to Philip's company, if he were free. I knew, almost superstitiously, that one should never go back, never retrace one's steps in the hope that all would be as before, for it never is. I had planned to return to Paris at a much later date, possibly in January or February when I should have noted all the references that needed to be checked, all the errors or omissions that must be rectified. That would have to be an extended stay, possibly into the late spring, which would allow me time for a few more studies on-site. This would be fairly intensive work and would brook no interruption. This weekend visit was premature, badly timed, and by now so irrelevant that I had almost managed to forget it. It was clear that I was not expected to stay any longer than any of the other guests. My task would be to go home as rapidly as possible and write to convey my thanks at a safe distance. And I should do that, I thought, wholeheartedly, not giving any hint that I had been anything other than gratified by the invitation. The letter, I knew, would be appreciated far more than my attendance would be.

'I have to go to France this weekend,' I told Philip, placing before him a perfect omelette.

'Where do you get this bread? It's rather good.'

'An Italian place up the road. Would you like me to get you a loaf?'

'No, no. This is fine.'

'I should be back on Monday. Or possibly Sunday night. I have no reason to stay.'

'You won't get much work done, then.'

'Some friends to see. What will you do?'

'Nothing much.'

'I'll see you next week, of course. You'll still be here?'

'Of course. Why shouldn't I be?'

'I need to know that I'll find everything as I left it. I now have faintly superstitious feelings about going away, although I never used to. I think perhaps I have been reconverted to Englishness. And yet I know that as soon as I get there I shall be reconverted in the opposite direction.'

'I never took to Paris myself, always wanted to press on to the south. Any south. I could never adapt to Parisians. I'm too dull, I expect.'

'So am I, really. But one learns so much by just being there, how to eat, how to dress. Flair.'

'It's no doubt different for a woman.'

'In fact I didn't learn all that well. Oh, the superficial things, perhaps. But I haven't the sort of temperament that adapts easily. Now I feel that the lessons are over, that I might have been too naïve to make the most of them, as if I had been a child when I first went there and have grown up since. And yet I know that when I get there I shall want to learn all over again. It's an eternal apprenticeship, trying to be like the French.'

I also knew that what was missing from our relationship was a festiveness, a cordiality that I had perhaps only absorbed at second hand, to be replaced by a feeling of safety that threatened to descend into acceptance. The scholarly disposition, to which I laid claim, is not necessarily innate; it develops in default of other aptitudes. I worried, as never before, that I might, almost certainly should, make a poor showing: I had misgivings not only about status but about worth. My friendship with Françoise now appeared to me lightweight, whereas I had thought to endow it with significance. This was also the verdict I now reached about my friendship with Michael. That had been the sort of friendship that children know, and although Philip did not appear to find me childish I knew that I had adapted too easily to his needs, without examining my own. The compliance that was my greatest weakness could only be alleviated by the illusion that I could suspend it whenever I chose. Now I saw that this was not the case. The solution was, once again, to leave home, and to learn whatever new lessons I was still capable of absorbing.

'Do you want to walk back with me?' he was saying.

'No, not tonight. I think I might leave in the morning. Yes, that might be best. I'll see you next week.'

'You seem anxious to be rid of me.'

'I'm only anxious to get there and back. If I stay much longer I might never move again.'

The desire to stay was threatened by the need to get away. The journey would be filled with a strange anxiety which I had not previously felt, as if I feared some ambush. I regretted Françoise's absence, she who had offered me protection of a kind. Or maybe I feared absence itself, an existential absence to which only philosophers have the key. In any event I was ill-equipped for a formal social occasion at which any kind of awkwardness would be unacceptable. I looked, once more, to Paris to supply me with certainties that I did not possess. The night was too long for me. By five a.m. I was out of the flat and on my way to Waterloo.

I took another room at the hotel, unwilling to engage in further discussion. There was a call for me, from a Mme Mauvoisin. Would I call back? This I did in the hope that the whole arrangement had been cancelled. Mme Mauvoisin's voice was brisk and decisive, but her assurance seemed to waver when she heard who I was and finally to collapse. She would be only too willing to drive to L'Ermitage, she said, but she ought to warn me that she would have to leave early, as soon after lunch as was decently possible. She would be accompanying her father who was very old and in poor health; also she was anxious to get home to her husband who was also not well and who disliked being left alone. I glanced out of the window at the brilliant day and wondered why these invalids thought fit to give this occasion priority over their own comfort, but this was to underestimate the social cohesiveness of the French bourgeoisie. I assured Mme Mauvoisin that I was more than grateful, not only to be driven down but to be returned to Paris as expeditiously as possible. This, if anything, caused her more concern, or perhaps she was pursuing her own line of thought. Her father, she went on to say, was an old friend of Mme Desnoyers, but she doubted his ability to mingle with strangers. He had occasional lapses of memory and she would have to keep a close eye on him. But as he hardly got out at all these days she felt she could not deny him this pleasure. She would be delighted to make my acquaintance and was grateful for my understanding. No questions were put to me but I felt obliged to explain that I was a friend of Françoise, at which her voice seemed even more doubtful. I thanked her, in advance, as it were, as if few words were to be wasted on the return journey, and said that I should be ready at the appointed time on the Sunday and assured her once again that I was more than happy to fit in with her plans. I did this for her sake as well as my own: clearly the subtext was one of polite reluctance on both sides.

It was a relief to get out into the street, where I was immediately revived by all the sights and sounds that had recently been missing from my life. The sun was high after a morning mist which had signalled autumn, and it was warm: at midday it would be hot. I drank my coffee in the bar next to the hotel and was gratified to be recognized by the owner. I was questioned about my absence: *bonnes vacances*? I enquired after his family and was assured that all were well. This minimal social exchange was so reassuring that I was encouraged to believe that I was not entirely a stranger here, rather less so, it seemed to me, than I was in London, where such salutations were more superficial. Almost automatically I set out for the library, although there was not much point in doing so, as I had left all my material in the flat. But I wanted to see if all was as before, if those obedient heads were still bent over their work, if the same peaceful atmosphere still reigned. I had nothing to do: I thought for conscience' sake I might look over an account of Fouquet's commission to Le Nôtre, and then, when I had satisfied myself that this had not changed since the last time I checked it, I might go to the Musée des Arts Décoratifs for another sight of those obelisks and fountain designs before issuing out into the brilliant day and restoring my sense of optimism, which had in fact been in place, tentatively at first and then with increasing depth, ever since I arrived, smelt the

coffee and the cigarettes, sidestepped the water thrown in an arc
to sluice the morning pavements, bought my newspaper, and
appreciated once more a lack of obligations, but also of recent
attachments, that impressed me as the freedom I might allow
myself to enjoy and which had been in eclipse for far too long.

I banished my recent misgivings, which I now saw as
morbid and unnecessary, an echo of fears which had nothing to
do with this bright day. Though others around me seemed as
purposeful as ever my own steps slowed in a sensuous appreciation of the light and the warmth and that blessed sense of
relief at being back where I felt strongest, bravest. I decided
to leave the museum to the following day, and walked in a
measured and unreflecting fashion to the Place Saint-Sulpice,
almost glad now that I knew no one well but all in a recognizable spirit of fraternity. It was only when the sun was obscured by a passing dullness, forerunner perhaps of the mist that
would once more descend towards evening, that I went again
into the great church, for a sight of those women in black,
come faithfully to record their requests—for health, for the future of a beloved son, for relief from pain—that retained their
validity even if the request were not granted. Such faith was
unknown to me; my life had to be lived pragmatically, and any
dislocations and disappointments made good out of my own
poor resources. I regretted this but accepted it as inevitable.
This was made possible by the surrounding urban splendour,
and plans were already forming in my head for a return which

might follow in due course and which I might prolong into a future for which I now felt a certain hope.

I was glad too that I had managed to settle, in some mysterious way, the business of Françoise's presence in the hotel, and felt bewildered that this had preoccupied me at such length and with so little purpose. Lightness was all. I should be able to greet her without a shadow, and she would know, from my genuine pleasure at seeing her, that she could do the same. But then she had always managed to do this; her ability went with the brightness of the air, the straightness of the streets, the ever-commanding perspectives of the city which she graced with such assurance. For a moment I was saddened by the contrast between her insouciance and my own laborious calculations, and on the heels of this came a slight failure of nerve. The day had invigorated me, but now there was the night to contend with, and ahead of me a long Saturday when I should be left without an illusion of company. This was the time of day when I could look forward to Philip's presence, though this was rarely announced in advance: he knew where to find me and acted accordingly. Already this had become customary, and I saw and was convinced of its advantages. That I was seeking some escape from it did not impress me: I saw this as natural.

When the sun was finally veiled I turned back to the hotel. In the distance I saw someone who looked like Michael— same red scarf, same untidy hair—but when he turned round it was clear that it was someone completely different.

15

'ON VOUS ATTEND EN BAS, MADEMOISELLE.'

I shivered in my thin jacket, having surmised, correctly as it turned out, that this was no occasion for off-duty English Sunday scruffiness. A white mist blanketed the window, foreclosing all but immediate perspectives. I had been ready for nearly an hour.

Mme Mauvoisin seemed equally constrained, as she led me out to the car. In the passenger seat sat an old man wrapped in what looked like a cashmere coat, with a muffler tied tightly round his neck. I inclined my head through the window.

'Emma Roberts,' I announced.

An ivory hand was passed out. '*Enchanté, Mademoiselle. Je connais très bien votre pays, New York, Washington. J'étais en poste à New York dans les années cinquante. J'étais très bien là-bas Connaissez-vous les Beckmann? Des gens adorables.*'

'*Monsieur, je suis anglaise.*'

'*Ah.*' His enthusiasm dwindled as he lost interest, apparently for all time, and turned his head away. Mme Mauvoisin laid a consoling hand on her father's arm and motioned me into the back of the car. A silence was observed which had less to do with this oddly formal occasion than with M. de Robillard's momentary humiliation, for which I was responsible. I felt for him, for his obvious disorientation, for this moment of feebleness of which he was too aware. As Mme Mauvoisin patted his arm in a gesture that was clearly habitual his face relaxed. We sat silent in the car, careful not to disturb him. Within a few minutes he had subsided into a light doze. Mme Mauvoisin and I exchanged a meaningful glance. The journey would be equally silent.

The familiar landscape was shrouded in the same white mist that had greeted me through the windows of my room, thickening as we left Paris and blanketing the countryside through which we passed swiftly. There seemed to be no other cars on the road, and few people. In the occasional village figures could be observed at the doors of churches. The sun, an even whiter blur, struggled unavailingly to break through. My heart went out, not only to M. de Robillard and his daughter, but to Mme Desnoyers whose entertainment seemed threatened by this uncompromising weather. My first sight of the house was an equally white blur at the end of a creaking road. Gravel crunched as we entered the drive. When the car drew up to take its place among several others, the sun made an effort and broke through. As if to signal that proceedings had begun, voices could be heard, and I could see, on the terrace, a small crowd of people, none of whom I recognized.

When M. de Robillard was extricated from the car and led over to Mme Desnoyers I saw those faces last encountered at that first evening at the house: Mme Dulong, Mme de Freyssinet, the Bachelards, and of course Mme de Lairac, who seemed to be as much the hostess as Mme Desnoyers herself. Their colour was high; they were onstage. Mme Desnoyers greeted me abstractedly and nodded her approval as I allowed M. de Robillard to take my arm. She herself seemed exalted: two spots of colour burned on her cheekbones and I was aware of her rasping breath. Again I felt a sadness that all this effort might have come too late. But then I saw Françoise, no longer in her usual black but in a smart Chanel jacket and short pleated skirt. She looked beautiful, gracious: she too was onstage.

We moved into the dining room, which had been transformed for the occasion: three round tables had been set up; the usual dining table had been pushed back against the wall and now held a large glistening salmon with cucumber scales, a Brie, a Vacherin, and a giant bowl of raspberries. Fernand, in his white jacket, stood stiffly to attention; two girls in blue overalls, acquaintances of his, or possibly relatives, awaited his orders. Mariette, who had brought the salmon to its state of perfection, was out of sight. We were assigned to our tables in no particular order. One was presided over by Mme Desnoyers, one by Françoise, and one by Jean-Charles de Lairac. The significance of this was lost on no one. No indication was given that this order of precedence had been noted, but it was equally significant that Mme de Lairac had judged it correct to abandon her usual place at her son's side and sit at Françoise's table, just as if she were merely another guest.

I was opposite Jean-Charles, who favoured me with the insistent stare by which he had first announced himself. He stood out, not because he was in any way remarkable, but because he was the only able-bodied man there. Indeed there were few men, so few that I had a woman on my left. On my right was M. de Robillard, who had started to tackle his bread as soon as he had sat down. On his right was his faithful daughter. At a sign from Mme Desnoyers, Fernand broke into the salmon, divided it into rather small portions, and sent the girls round with the plates. Clearly no expense had been spared. I was relieved that I was not as unsuitably dressed as usual, and tried to enjoy myself. This was not easy. I was cold, the salmon was cold, and at one point M. de Robillard's *petit pain* shot off his plate and landed in my lap. Fortunately no one had noticed, not even M. de Robillard himself.

I could just see the back of Françoise's head. She was in conversation with another elderly man, at what I thought of as the grown-ups' table. She had given no sign of recognition other than the bright smile with which she had greeted me. I was doubly grateful for the knowledge that I should be returned to Paris fairly soon and resolved, if possible, to catch a late train back to London.

The lady on my left, to whom I had paid little attention, now engaged me in conversation. I had perhaps overlooked her owing to my supervisory duties with M. de Robillard, but also, it has to be said, because of her eager humble expression: a poor relation, I had concluded, whose role was to be Mme Desnoyers's loyal admirer. This was almost the case. She introduced herself as Aline Mercier, and said she was a neighbour. But she was also a relation, if not necessarily a close one: her grandmother and Mme Desnoyers's grandmother had been sisters. She had lost touch with Mme Desnoyers until she had moved to this part of the world on the death of her husband, anxious to be near someone she knew, or knew of, since she had no children. She told me all this in a light insistent voice which needed no response from me: indeed there was little I could make, since she seemed intent on bringing me up to date with her affairs. Her husband had been ill for many months, she said, and after his death the flat had been too big for her and she was lonely. It was she who suggested moving to Sucy-en-Brie, although she had no intention of underlining the family connection. But wasn't Françoise a lovely girl? I agreed. Mme Mercier's face shone with affection and with a sort of proprietary longing, from which I deduced that she was not a frequent guest at L'Ermitage, although qualified, perhaps, by her very eagerness, her humility. Clearly she had not done well for herself, or not as well as Mme Desnoyers. Their common background may have been humbler than Mme Desnoyers would have cared to admit. She had been introduced to me as *'Aline Mercier, la plus fidèle des amies'*, acknowledging her but not identifying her. Mme Mercier had offered a grateful smile, accepting without question the relegation from relation to acquaintance. Of the whole gathering she appeared to be enjoying herself possibly more than anyone else in the room.

In the larger of the two salons the long windows had been opened on to what was now a brilliant day. Few, however, ventured out onto the terrace. I took my place next to M. de Robillard and was soon joined by Mme Mercier. I felt like a child between two parents, and made an effort to sit up straight. My inclination was to relax entirely, now that I knew I had acquitted myself with due propriety, but a glance at the rest of the company told me that if any of the other guests felt a mild slackening of their attention this was not apparent. Fortunately the meal had not been lavish enough to induce sleepiness. At my side Mme Mercier, who seemed willing to endow our brief acquaintance with all the goodwill at her command, continued her roll call of appreciations in her curiously penetrating voice, to which I responded encouragingly, though no encouragement was needed. Françoise, passing by, gave me a brilliant smile, in which there was a tremor of complicity. A slight shift in Mme Mauvoisin's taut posture was the sign that she was anxious to leave. As, it seemed, were one or two of the other guests, too well-mannered to linger, but willing to take their leave in as elaborate a fashion as seemed decreed by the beautiful room, the sun which had endowed the occasion with the ultimate accolade, and the figure of Mme Desnoyers as she continued her own appreciative comments directed indiscriminately at her friends, most of whom had now risen from their chairs. Jean-Charles, I was interested to note, had rejoined his mother, as if this were a natural pairing, but I also noted the casual expertise with which he assessed my appearance and the decisiveness with which he signalled to one of the maids to remove his mother's precipitantly balanced coffee cup. This she did meekly, as if it were customary.

I was already composing my letter, in my best Cornelian French, as I took my leave of Mme Desnoyers. Here I was overshadowed by the warmth of Mme Mercier's salutations, as well as by M. de Robillard's reminiscences. The guests were queueing up, as at a wedding reception, for now a general exodus had been agreed upon. Mme Desnoyers greeted everyone as if they had just arrived. It struck me, and perhaps others, that she was not quite well. Her spirits were unflagging, her attention unrelenting, but her colour was too high, her breath effortful. Sheer discipline, which I could only admire, kept her on her feet. Françoise, equally determined, took her place at her mother's side. She managed to say that she was so glad to see me and that she would telephone later that evening, but I told her that I should be leaving for London and would talk to her soon. Fixed in my mind was the image of my quiet flat, where I suddenly longed to be. Then I was out in the blessed air. The weather, as if to indicate closure, had dulled down and the mist was rising. I stood by the car, while M. de Robillard was led back inside, presumably to a bathroom. Around me cars started up, but there was no cordial raising of voices. Propriety reigned. There had not been a single note of intimacy in the entire proceedings.

The journey back to Paris was conducted in silence, in deference to M. de Robillard's light slumber. I was grateful for this. I was feeling mildly alienated, as if the whole affair had taken place in a time warp, or in a *fête galante* by Watteau or Fragonard. It was quite easy to transpose those guests into one of those colloquies in which nothing is explicit but in which ritual exchanges take place. In many of those images there is an outsider, a figure in harlequin costume: a hand is laid on a breast; one assumes that love, or something more savage, is in the air. There had been none of this at L'Ermitage. Even the presumed lovers had behaved like obedient children. What had been missing, I now realized, was that spark, that hint of lubricity which the whole assembly would have recognized, perhaps with an indulgent smile. Instead there had been a courtliness that was merely dull. One had to admire, as I was sure not only I did, the extreme discipline which kept everyone playing their part. And yet the radiant artificiality of Françoise, the ironic assiduity of Jean-Charles, were somehow disturbing. I preferred my old friend in her more iconoclastic moments, or as I had first seen her in the library, dispensing a generous gaiety towards mild-mannered strangers, gratifying them with her not quite mocking attention before they turned their minds to more exacting study. I wished with all my heart that she would manage to save her own life from the conformity that threatened her. It takes a kind of genius to save one's own life, the sort of genius that I so signally lacked. But if Françoise, who possessed that kind of genius, could manage to extricate herself from the trap which those ferocious parents had devised, I was sure that there would be a quiet and secret smile of commendation on the part of those who would be publicly scandalized.

Mme Mauvoisin dropped me back at the hotel, which was kind of her since she lived near the Parc Monceau. Again we thanked each other warmly, but in lowered voices: M. de Robillard was not to be disturbed. I stood on the pavement until the car moved away, half-wishing that she had had a mind to prolong the exchange. I longed to discuss what I had seen, and suddenly missed my mother, who would have enjoyed every detail. I was tired; the whole event had been a strain, exactly as I had anticipated. In fact my feelings had been premonitory. Although nothing dreadful had happened I had been prepared for dangers that had not materialized, and this had coloured my appreciation of what had been a purely formal, purely decorative occasion. Any uneasiness I had felt had been my own affair. I turned into the hotel with none of the relief that I should have felt. There seemed little point in either staying or leaving. The letter I should write as soon as I was back in London would be a masterpiece of insincerity. But that was quite in order, for insincerity had been the keynote throughout the day.

My most conscious need was for air, for exercise, for a long walk. I felt as if I had been in too rarefied an atmosphere for far too long. Did those people ever wander about, ruminative, unreflecting, unmotivated? Or, what was more likely, were they always under strict control, even on Sundays? The English Sunday was an amiable affair, unstructured, unsupervised, underdressed. The idea of sitting up straight and making polite conversation belonged in a foreign setting untouched by satire. Neither mode was particularly enjoyable; both were, in their different ways, accepted without question. The fact that Sundays were always slightly disappointing was more or less taken for granted.

Since there was nothing to detain me I took a cab to the station. Through the window I viewed the normal Sunday activities, unassuming people strolling, looking in shop windows, issuing from museums, activities in which I had once joined. My return to this place suddenly seemed problematic, devoid of context. Despite the expertise of the behaviour I had recently witnessed I felt discomforted. How was I now to greet Françoise, from whom all spontaneity had been removed? I was used to her as a cynical guide, ready to take on the world, alive to her mother's subterfuges and determined to resist them. Now I saw that she was more like her mother than I had divined, that she had gone over to the side of people whose cynicism was in fact superior to her own. I had been a guest whose appreciation could be counted on but who was not supposed to have an opinion, a subordinate with no function other than that of standing by. I did not underestimate their kindness in inviting me, and indeed had been aware of my steady smile, for nothing less would be appropriate, but it was as if I had been present at a Sunday matinée at the Comédie Française, at which one took one's place in the audience, duly admiring the strophe and antistrophe, and relieved when it was time to leave one's seat and get back to one's less than noble life. Perhaps I had more in common than I realized with Aline Mercier, grateful for the attention, a part she played to perfection. The excellence of her performance, which had seemed perfectly sincere, derived from the fact that she had grown old in the part. The danger was that I might do the same.

Yet she must at one time have protested that she too had a view on the matter in hand, which I now saw as cold in the extreme. Part of me railed against the loveless spectacle of those so gracious people acceding to a merger of two undisguised interests, and most of all at Françoise's transformation from lawless adventurer to potential upholder of the established order. On what terms would we now be friends? I had witnessed too much of her previous behaviour to take her present persona on trust, was too used to her as rough guide to the real world to adjust my attitude to one of unrealistic acceptance. The only ray of hope, as I saw it, was the existence of the American lover, and the part he would have to play in this comedy of manners. Unthinkable though it might be, I hoped that he would have a voice in the proceedings, might reduce the comedy to farce by the sheer force of his democratic insistence. I remembered Françoise in her mother's bedroom, watching that American soap opera with an unaccustomed expression of longing, subdued, impressed by the extravagant behaviour which her mother had so haughtily condemned. Was that what she really wanted, the freedom to indulge a lower nature that had been (and still was) subject to fierce correction? I hoped that she really loved this unknown lover, if only to introduce that touch of nature that had been so awfully lacking in her mother's plans. That mother, seduced by the prospect of a flat in Paris and a new life, had had her own freedom to consider. It would be interesting, though not comfortable, to watch these two imperatives battling it out.

The train was filled with people reading the Sunday papers, the scene once again recognizably English. The man sitting next to me kindly handed me the *Telegraph,* seeing that I had nothing with me. I thanked him; I was in fact touched that I had been noticed, but hoped that no conversation would be necessary. I read studiously, without taking in a single word, regretting Sundays past, even regretting that laconic lunch at the Hyde Park Hotel, at which I had been allowed to speak my mind without damaging results. And those other Sundays, which were gone forever. I wondered whether I might ring Philip when I got back to the flat. I had a sudden desire to see him, but realized that it was late, and that his son might be there. As the train eased itself into Waterloo the man beside me retrieved his various possessions and said, 'You're travelling light, then.' 'Oh, yes,' I replied. 'I go back and forth a lot. I shall be back in Paris very soon.' But that seemed a far cloudier prospect now than it had ever done in the past.

16

THERE WAS NO REPLY TO MY LETTER, WHICH DID NOT surprise me. What did surprise me was that there was no communication from Françoise, whose side of the story I longed to hear. But perhaps she had passed into another sphere, which took no account of earlier confessions. These were now cancelled by her apparently new status, one she had assumed confidently, in a manner which seemed to preclude intimacy. She was, after all, her mother's daughter; and I, my own reclusive mother's daughter, remained the recipient of what she chose to tell me, not quite happy in my role but resigned to it nonetheless.

Slightly more puzzling, though not in any sense disturbing, was the absence of Philip. We had made no arrangements to see each other, for the essence of the whole affair was an informality that verged on absentmindedness. I almost forgot about him until shocked into remembered pleasure when he turned up. I assumed that he felt the same. This was no love affair, but it was an acceptable union between two people whose feelings may not have been immediately available to them. I liked him: that was how I put it to myself, without pursuing the matter. I accepted the proposition that eternal vigilance is the price of liberty, and held myself in readiness for the time when that liberty, which I only partly enjoyed, should turn into something more compelling, should turn, in fact, into a fate that I should recognize as inevitable. I had only to wait. In the meantime I told myself that I was sufficiently comfortable with the situation to wish it to continue. It had taught me some valuable lessons, chief of which was not to ask too many questions. If this imposed a certain reserve, a certain formality, I saw that this was more acceptable than my initial forays into loquacity. In fact a degree of silence, while in no way restricting, suited us both. I felt I knew his tastes and habits well enough, and absolved myself from further study. This restful condition was almost homely, as if it had lasted for a very long time, as if it rested on established fact. I believe this condition of unwarranted confidence to be a mild mental disorder, but this did not at the time strike me as unusual.

It was the disappearance of the sun that ushered in a duller perspective. One always hopes, consciously or unconsciously, for a welcome, or at least an acknowledgement of one's existence. Now the days were creeping towards the annual darkness; the mist, which had previously seemed only a prelude to a radiance, however brief, had thickened into a fog which blanketed the early mornings and did not lift until nearly midday. I went out grudgingly, with only a brief 'Good morning' to interrupt the silence that seemed to have settled even on this busy neighbourhood. My purchases seemed futile; the mild sense of ceremony had evaporated, and I could see myself as going through the motions of preparing for another's presence. Also I disliked the false air of domesticity that I had assumed. I was out of character here, as if only displacement could bring out my carefully cultivated self-sufficiency. In the hotel, in the library, I was at one with all those famous exiles who had eventually triumphed over circumstances. It was, paradoxically, the knowledge that one had voluntarily cut oneself off from one's roots that brought about the liberating courage to persist, to seek one's continuity in those who followed a similar trajectory. I had few friends in London, even among those I had known all my life, but the librarian, the bartender, the concierge were people on whom I could count for a sense of permanence which reassured me. As the weather changed, the flat seemed to grow darker, more silent, and it was no longer comfortable to spend much time there. Even the streets failed me. Christmas decorations were already in evidence in shop windows, 'seasonal' delicacies already on the shelves of supermarkets. I longed for open country, where weather could be properly evaluated. I longed for a proper visit to L'Ermitage, and a long walk with Françoise through the woods. Short of that I missed the illusion of comfort bestowed by a visit from Philip and his ability to dispel the terrors of the night.

His eventual reappearance therefore was coloured by a certain awkwardness, even apprehension. I was not mistaken about this: I knew the signs too well, the preemptive smile that verged on jocularity, the solicitude, the excessive greeting. This was not the sort of behaviour I had come to expect from Philip, and I thought it diminished him slightly. But I put this reaction aside in the sheer relief I felt at his presence. I could not, however, help noticing his appearance, which had been amended, not altogether favourably. He wore a lightweight cream linen suit which was not appropriate and had subjected himself to a severe haircut. I preferred him in his usual off-duty uniform of nondescript twill trousers and a tweed jacket. Nevertheless I appreciated the fact that he had made an effort, though the effort did not entirely become him. He was more impressive in his usual role: abstracted, withdrawn, attentive but not indulgent. I wondered if I appeared to him as nervous as I suddenly felt. I poured the wine, which we both seemed to need.

'You're looking very smart,' I said. The 'smart' seemed almost accusatory, containing more criticism than appreciation.

'I'm taking my wife out to dinner.'

'Ah. I see. I thought you were divorced.'

'No, we never got divorced. There was always the

possibility—or I hoped there was—that we might get back to-gether again.'

'I do so envy married couples. Even when they fall out they retain that possibility of retreating into safety.'

'It is not always safety.'

'No, of course not. But you are allowed to misbehave. It is even a convention.'

'I thought we got along pretty well, you and I.'

'That's because I was always on my best behaviour.'

'You once said you didn't have a best.'

'This is as good as it gets.'

'There's no reason why we shouldn't meet from time to time.'

'Oh, I think there is. I no longer like the position I'm in.'

'I gave you no reason to hope. . . .'

'No, you didn't. Maybe that was the worst of it.'

'You are an attractive woman, Emma.'

'Woman? I felt like a girl, waiting to be chosen. Grateful when I thought I was. There's nothing anyone can do about this: it must be inbred in the female condition. All the brave talk that women have learned to spout doesn't alter this.'

'I'm sorry if you thought otherwise.'

'It has almost nothing to do with you.'

There was a pause.

'I always hoped that we might be a family again.'

'I can understand that perfectly well. I too should have

liked to be a family. Which is rather difficult if you are on your own.'

'Yes, I feel for you there. But we were never on those terms. I too have felt lonely.'

'I think that was the most attractive thing about you. I thought that we were keeping each other company.'

'We were.'

'But you have better company now. Or might have. That will be your priority now.'

'As I say, there is no reason why we shouldn't . . .'

'You are making a poor job of this, Philip. Or no, it is I who am making a poor job of it. I should have behaved well, as people are supposed to do in these circumstances, offered only polite comments, poured you another glass of wine. Wished you luck. Assured you of my distinguished sentiments, as they say in France.'

'Well, I know where you are. I'll keep in touch. As a friend.'

'You have always known where to find me. That perhaps was reassuring for both of us. But I can't promise to be here anymore. I'll go back to Paris, of course. There's no reason why I shouldn't stay there.'

'You have your work, of course.'

'My alibi. It's what I say I do when people ask me. It's a question I'm always having to answer. That's another reason to envy married couples. There is no question mark over them, as there is over people like myself. They are their own alibi. I see every reason why you and your wife should get together again.'

'She may not want me.'

'Then she is a very foolish woman.'

There was another pause.

'As I say, I made no promises. We were not on those terms, you and I.'

'No, you are in the clear, technically at least. I have enjoyed your company.'

'And I yours.'

'Goodbye, Philip. You will be late for your dinner.'

'You are going too far. My wife may not agree to this. She always found me rather dull.'

'You are not dull. A little secretive, perhaps.'

'I'm sorry, Emma. As I say, we can always see each other from time to time.'

'No, I don't think so.'

'When will you go back to Paris?'

'Tomorrow morning.' I held out my hand. I felt he wanted me to wish him luck. 'Good luck,' I said. I hated the plucky words. I really did wish him well, but could think of no more sensible way of saying so. I had said too much already, and I knew that my own words would haunt me. Although I could not have suppressed them I saw with hideous clarity how I could have saved the day, agreed to a compromise, acquiesced in whatever arrangements he cared to propose. Quite simply I had not done so, and thus had sealed my own fate. I was not even pleased with myself for showing a modicum of moral courage, for moral cowardice would have served me better. It would also have been more welcome in the circumstances, or whatever the circumstances turned out to be. It was my isolation that had so unwisely spoken, when isolation is never a good card to play. And perhaps I had perceived an insult where none was intended. I had no experience to guide me. Even this particular experience was of little use.

I heard his footsteps going down the street but did not go to the window for a last look at his retreating back. I sat where I was for perhaps half an hour and then went into the bedroom to pack my bag. Once again I should leave at dawn, but this time with the knowledge that I might not return.

The journey was peaceful, my arrival unnoticed. I was grateful to the hotel people for not enquiring how long I intended to stay; by now it was taken for granted that the current arrangements, for both myself and Françoise, would continue indefinitely. I knew that she would not question this, and that too was a comfort. We could revert to our former friendship without the need for further discussion. I was conscious of a feeling of failure which threatened to become endemic. I should pay dearly for my flash of resentment, which now seemed to be entirely unjustified. Outside my window I could hear confident footsteps, cheerful exchanges. This was the matrix into which I should have to embed myself. But a change had taken place.

Although always circumspect, obedient to established codes of conduct, I felt anxious to experience more intimacy than I had previously been allowed. Maybe that was the reason for my frank speaking; maybe the liberty afforded by such words had been irresistible. If Philip and I were to resume our former relationship I should probably have to renounce such transparency. I felt like someone who has impulsively resigned from a job and wonders how to reapply without losing face. For the moment there was nothing to be done. The best tactic was to let time pass. This now felt like true exile, in comparison with which former fantasies disintegrated.

Françoise's eyes widened when I entered the library. There had been a change there too. She seemed unduly thoughtful, limiting her cheerful enquiries to a subdued murmur which may have been a disappointment to those who secretly cherished her rallying scorn. On her second round of the desks she tapped her watch and nodded slightly in the direction of the door. This meant midday at the Café des Amis. There was little point in settling down. I went round the corner to wait for her, relieved that this custom at least had not changed. This was homecoming of a sort, and the relief was almost palpable. Yet I knew, by osmosis, perhaps, by telepathy, that she was as distracted as I was. That she was genuinely glad to see me was also clear.

She sat down heavily, like a much older woman. 'I shall miss this,' she said. 'I'm glad you came.'

'Has something happened?'

'I've given in my notice. I said I'd stay until they appointed someone else. I shall miss that too.'

'The room is paid for until the end of the year. After that . . .'

'After that I shall be married.'

'It's all settled, then?'

She took a packet of cigarettes from her bag, but left it on the table. 'Not quite. Bill—my friend—wants me to go back to America with him. He won't accept the fact that this is impossible. There is no point in trying to explain. They do things differently in America.'

'What will you do?'

'I shall be with him as much as I can.'

'You love him.' It was not a question.

'Yes. I was not prepared for this. I thought the future would take care of itself.'

'Will you tell your mother that you have resigned?'

'No, of course not. I must have a reason for staying in Paris. Though she needs me. She is not well, Emma; the party was too much for her. She was successful in what she set out to do, but she has paid the price. She had a mild attack after they had all gone, but being my mother she managed to wait until we were alone together.'

'What sort of an attack?'

She smiled faintly. 'You will see for yourself when you come down. You will come, won't you? This weekend?'

'But if she is not well . . .'

'She is very fond of you, you know. It will do her good to see you. She is alone with the servants most of the time, and they are finding it difficult. But she knows that she must do nothing to annoy them.'

'She too has changed, then.'

'Most of all. More than anyone. But we hope that she will make a full recovery.'

'Why not tell her about Bill?'

'It would be too dangerous. She needs to know that everything will go ahead as planned. Besides, I have never confided in her. That is not our way.'

'Are you sure I won't be a nuisance?'

'Quite sure. It may not be as comfortable as usual, but I should be glad of your company. She keeps to her room most of the time. We are all under strain, the servants most of all. They are not young, and Fernand finds the stairs difficult.'

'If I can help in any way . . .'

'Just talk to her. Be cheerful. And we can have a long walk: I need that. I need to be away from the house for a bit.'

'You must resign yourself to being there a great deal in the future. Unless . . .'

'Unless. Will you be free to leave on Friday? Or sooner,

perhaps. They owe me some time at the library. They have been very good. Could you go tomorrow?'

'Of course.'

'Then I'll see you in the morning.' The sardonic boldness which had formerly defined her features had dissolved into a mature sadness. She was marked by love, in a way that I had not been. It had not made her happy. 'I have no friends, you see,' she said suddenly. 'No women friends, that is. I never thought I should need them.'

'You've got me.'

She smiled. 'Until tomorrow.'

We were as one, perhaps, in the knowledge that the future had failed us, that life had not proceeded in the straight line on which we had once relied. Such knowledge is not desirable, and is moreover impossible to impart to those untouched by it. 'Reader, I married him,' says Jane Eyre, in the most accessible line in English fiction. This should be the end of the journey for everyone: it is accepted as such, even by sceptics. Françoise's case was more serious than my own, and I could only admire her stoicism. Not a word of complaint passed her lips on the journey down; only her profile showed signs of a fatigue that came from deep inside her. It was in silence that we unpacked the car, took the shopping we had done in Paris into the kitchen, greeted a wary Fernand and Mariette, and went out onto the terrace to prepare for our participation in whatever

had been decided for us, or whatever manipulation of circumstances could be contrived.

My first sight of Mme Desnoyers was not as bad as I had
anticipated. It was true that the drooping eyelid obscured her
right eye, and that her greeting to me was unclear. 'Emma,' she
managed to say, before renouncing the attempt to say more.
She was seated in the smaller of the two salons, and formally
dressed, though without that air of activity that she had always
commanded. I pressed her hand, which remained limply in my
own. I tactfully left the room, after having mimed my delight at
being in her house again, and, naturally, at seeing her looking
so well. Françoise followed me out. She too pressed my hand.
'I'll stay with her for a while,' she said. 'You don't mind? Have
a walk, why don't you? I'll see you at lunch.'

I walked, reluctantly at first, later with relief. Trees dripped
steadily with the last of the mist, or the fog: it was hard to make
out in the midst of the woods. I wanted to become as tired as
possible so as not to think too much, to get through this awkward time without too much speculation. It was with growing
reluctance that I turned back to the house. I had managed to
kill only an hour and a half.

Lunch was the quiche we had brought from Paris. There
did not appear to be any other food; at least there was none on
the table. Mme Desnoyers had been returned to her room,
where she spent the rest of the day. I appreciated the effort she
had made in greeting me. There was nothing for me to do, after

clearing the dishes, but to go out again. Later I sat on the damp terrace, wishing I had brought a book. Françoise did not re-appear. My last image of her, when I went in to say good night to Mme Desnoyers, was of a submissive figure, on a low stool, manicuring her mother's nails. The image, I knew, would stay with me for months, possibly years to come.

17

I WOKE LATE, TO THE SOUND OF VOICES RAISED IN ARGU-
ment, or protest, coming from downstairs. It seemed tactful to
stay in my room, though I was anxious to know how the day
was to proceed. I was anxious, above all, to get back to Paris.
I could not do this without Françoise, for I had no means of
transport. I should, I thought, ask her for the telephone number of a taxi firm, if there was such a thing in this outlying spot.
I must do this as casually as possible; it would not do to convey
my reluctance to remain here. I could clearly be of no further
use, and anyway her own duties, however unappealing, would
claim all her attention. She might be glad to be rid of me,
grateful that I had made the decision to leave of my own ac-
cord. Now that I had seen the situation for myself it was clear
that my presence would only be a distraction.

When the voices were silent I made my way downstairs,
wondering if I might ask for a cup of coffee. I found the
kitchens, which I had never visited before, but no sign of Fer-

nand, or of Mariette. On a table were the remains of the quiche, still on the original plate. In the scullery a tap dripped. A small radio, which could occasionally be heard in the upstairs rooms, stood silent. As I lingered there, unwilling to call out, Mariette marched through and removed it. She went out, paying me no attention. She then marched back, took a jar of instant coffee from a cupboard, put it on the table in front of me, and went out again. This, I deduced, was the limit of her obligation to me. No words were offered. She nodded as I thanked her, and disappeared, forever, it seemed. Here too I was out of place. I drank the coffee hastily, and went upstairs to wait for Françoise, of whom there was no sign, though hers had been one of the voices. Now there was silence, and no movement discernible anywhere.

I had more than enough time to notice that the weather had deteriorated. A thin rain was falling, making the house dark. On my last visit the French windows had been open, ready for the sun, which had obediently, if briefly, blazed. Now all was sodden and forbidding. I should have been glad of a sound, of traffic, perhaps, but there was none. Françoise's car, under a dripping tree, had acquired a few wet leaves plastered to its roof and windscreen. She too would be eager to leave this place, which now seemed deserted. A lost domain, I had thought it, but one which had been stripped of its legendary allure. I noticed that a few drops of rain had penetrated a window embrasure and lay on the sill, reflecting the leaden sky outside. It was only nine o'clock, and yet it seemed as if dusk was already approaching.

A sudden flurry of footsteps heralded the approach of Françoise, who was wearing a coat, as if preparing to go out. She looked flushed, harassed. 'You've had coffee?' she enquired. 'Good. Now listen, Emma, I have to go to Paris. Oh, don't look so worried. I'll be back later, this evening at the latest. You can stay the night, can't you?'

'What's happened?'

'My friend wants to see me. I telephoned him late last night. This may be the last chance we have to be together. He leaves in a couple of days; the date has been brought forward. This is our last chance to discuss things. I have to go. You do see that, don't you?'

'Can't I come with you?'

'Well, no. As I say, I shall be back later. The servants will look after you. Fernand will see to my mother; there is no need for you to do anything. Just look in on her once or twice. I gave her a sleeping pill last night; she will probably sleep for most of the day. And then I'll take over.'

'I think you should stay,' I said. 'I have no experience. . . .'

'It's only for a few hours. I don't think it's too much to ask. As I say, you will be taken care of.' She glanced out of the window. 'Not a very nice day for a walk. Perhaps you could get down to some work. Make some notes, or something.'

'Is he really leaving so soon? Couldn't you prevail on him to stay?'

'That is what I am trying to do. It's my last chance.' I was silent. 'I would do the same for you,' she said, though there was no possibility of this, as we both knew. In my place she would find the situation intriguing, amusing, would give me every encouragement. There was no way of impeding her urgency, her desire not merely to get away but to be somewhere else at this very moment. It would be like trying to arrest a natural force, or dismantle a process that was almost complete. Even as she reassured me she kept glancing towards the door, as if only I were standing in her way, as if I were squandering her precious time. I felt careful, cautious, clumsy. It was only a few hours, after all. And if the weather cleared up I might venture out, explore the environs. This at least would take up the morning.

When the sound of the car died away I stood irresolute for a few minutes; clearly I had to reassure everyone that nothing had changed, though I was aware that it had, or that something had. I went up to Mme Desnoyers's room and knocked on the door. There was no answer. I looked in, but as Françoise had predicted, she was deeply asleep, her head fallen sideways on the pillow, her mouth open. Her breath was steady, steadier than I had ever heard it. I straightened the sheet. I had never performed such services before: my own mother had died without me, in a crowded place, among strangers. These duties were hers by right, or should have been, if she had waited for me. I was an impostor here, not quite an attendant, even less a daughter. And I was so clearly superfluous that my presence was not noticed. But the demands of the helpless are so powerful that I felt constrained to sit by the bed, in case she woke and wondered what had happened. It was only when Fernand came in and opened the window that I left. He could replace me, as no doubt Françoise had instructed. In the dining room a place had been laid and the quiche reassembled. This was lunch, well ahead of time, obviating the need for further contact.

It was clear that my presence in the house was unwelcome, and that it was questioned by the servants who seemed not merely indifferent, but hostile. I wandered out again into the woods, now dripping with moisture and silent except for the odd leaf falling onto the bed of leaves already fallen and forming a damp and slippery mat under my feet. I walked until I reached a clearing, where an iron gate marked the limit of the property. I turned back and forked left until I came to a road, which would be dusty in the summer but was now mud. It seemed imperative to find some sort of activity, some sign that this was a normal day in a normal part of the world, but all I could see was some sort of farm building in a distant field. I understood Mme Desnoyers's desire to relinquish this place, understood too her choice of friends, who were not friends in the normal understanding of the word but merely acquaintances or neighbours, willing to get into their cars and sacrifice an evening, on the understanding that she would do the same in return. I understood, even more clearly, Françoise's own desire, and the deliverance she sought from the rules which had stifled her throughout her upbringing and which now threatened to imprison her for the rest of her life. I even understood the suburban depths of my own soul, now longing for pavements and streetlights and the windows on to which I looked out from behind my own. This sudden feeling of displacement was radical; my life was circumscribed because I accepted that it should be. Occasional visits from a part-time lover were perhaps all that I could tolerate. Even those distant Sunday excursions with Michael were cherished because they came within safe limits, and those gardens I so faithfully studied were valued because they existed in a finite space and a time that could not be replicated. They would be dealt with, of course, for that was my mission and I should remain faithful to it. As I turned back to retrace my steps along the deserted road I knew that I should not come to this place again, that this particular episode was concluded, and that, if I ever thought of it, it would take on the dimensions of a romantic fantasy, one that I should be careful not to disturb.

I reckoned that Françoise would be back at about eight o'clock, nine at the latest. Inside the house, which now felt distinctly chilly, I could hear the muted sound of the radio, pre-

sumably restored to its place in the kitchen from the private
quarters that housed Fernand and his wife. I thought I should
signify my return in some way: I went down to the kitchen,
where Fernand and Mariette were seated at the table before
bowls of soup. They were listening to some sort of phone-in,
and I motioned them to continue their meal, which they did,
as if I were not there. When the soup bowls were emptied one
more was found for me, and filled. *'Mademoiselle est servie,'* said
Fernand ironically. Then the radio was switched off and once
again removed. In the ensuing silence I could hear their voices,
raised once again, from their distant quarters at the back of the
house. Again, some notion of an argument filtered through. I
left my soup bowl and went back upstairs. I was determined to
leave the next morning, as early as possible, with or without
Françoise. Unfortunately I had forgotten to ask her where I
could locate a taxi, or even hire a car. Short of this I should
have to find a bus, if one existed. Escape was now a priority.

In Mme Desnoyers's room Fernand had closed the shut-
ters, signifying that he envisaged no further duties that day. She
did not seem to have moved from her original position, but the
effect of the sleeping draught may have been wearing off, for
she was showing some signs of agitation. Françoise had evidently given her something which had kept her acquiescent;
now, inopportunely, she had begun to wake. At one stage her
good eye opened and located me, focused, and blazed briefly
with hauteur, as if I were an intruder. I assured her that Fran-

çoise was on her way, would be home very soon. She continued to stare at me indignantly, until her energy faltered, the eye closed, and she appeared to sleep.

I stayed with her a while longer, glancing repeatedly at my watch. I went into Françoise's bedroom, which was adjacent to that of Mme Desnoyers, and where I knew there was a telephone. I had only once been in this room, but remembered it as being as neat as that of a convent girl. Now the cupboard doors were open, and it seemed as if some clothes had been removed. I dialled the number of the hotel and asked to be put through to my old room. I let the telephone ring until I was convinced that she was not there. Then I dialled again and asked for her at the reception desk. No, they had not seen her, the concierge said, but she had been in at midday to collect her things. She had not been seen since then.

It was clear that she did not wish to be found. She might, almost certainly would, return, if only to set me free, perhaps later tonight. This now seemed unlikely: possible but unlikely. I had only to settle down, in Françoise's room, near the telephone, in case she called, and everything could be resolved. Even now I was more or less sympathetic to her plight, for when I was gone she would be alone with her mother, her dream of flight dashed, or revealed in all its fragility. It had been a brave attempt, but an unlikely one. At least, that was how my pragmatic nature argued. There remained the problem of her absence, though that might still prove temporary. I lay down on the bed, as tired as if I had tried to escape myself, and been foiled. I may have dozed, though it was too early to sleep. There was complete silence. The only noises I heard were in my head, dreams, or echoes of dreams. At some point, when the room was completely dark, I knew that she was not coming back.

When the chill rainy light once more managed to penetrate the room I rang the hotel again, and again an hour later. There was no change. I went down to the kitchens, where once more voices were raised, as they would not have been in the presence of the legitimate owners. Now a laxness was perceptible, as if they had abandoned all formality. They had reached the same conclusion as I had, but more speedily. Once again the jar of instant coffee was placed in front of me, the radio removed, and the room vacated. I returned to Françoise's room and rang the hotel again; now the response sounded frankly testy. I went in to Mme Desnoyers, willing her to be asleep. She was in fact in the process of struggling out of consciousness, but with evident difficulty. I laid my hand on hers and told her that Françoise would soon be back. The sound of the name was enough to agitate her, and she uttered sounds that signified, *Françoise! Françoise!* I stayed until she was quiet again, then left her, and telephoned the hotel once more. A slight commotion sent me to the window. Two hunched figures, carrying a heavy suitcase between them, were making their way round to the back of the house. It was as I feared: the servants, leaving.

My problems were now unlimited. I was determined not to spend another night in this place. I was tired and bewildered: I had not taken off my clothes for what seemed like an age but was in fact only one night. There was the overriding problem of how to look after Mme Desnoyers, who had not, as far as I knew, eaten anything for some time. Yet again I went down to the kitchen. On the table I found a bowl of eggs and a packet of *biscottes,* left by Mariette as a token of good faith. In an enormous pan which I found in the range I scrambled two of the eggs and took the resultant mess upstairs with me. Mme Desnoyers looked at me blankly. I spooned the eggs carefully into her mouth, and watched helplessly as they ran out again, until some reflex reminded her how to eat and she managed to swallow. I helped her to drink a little water, though most of that too escaped, and settled her, I hoped, for a rest. She made no protest, taking me for a nurse, or for a servant whom she did not remember employing. I had lost all sense of time, which may have been providential. This was a day like no other. I took the plate away, ate a couple of dry *biscottes,* and went back to Françoise's room, to wait.

When the telephone rang I took a precious few seconds to rid myself of my mounting indignation, and reached it just in time, a sign no doubt that in some other dimension providence was active on my behalf.

'Allo? Françoise? Ici, Aline. Françoise?'

Aline Mercier, *la plus fidèle des amies,* as Mme Desnoyers had described her, and the only one to contact her to ask if she might be of service.

'Madame,' I said. 'I am Emma Roberts. Do you remember? We met at that delightful lunch party a little while ago.'

The remembered voice softened. *'Mais oui, bonjour. Vous passez le weekend au château?'* For it had become a château, and perhaps always had been in her eyes.

I managed to summon up the requisite pleasantries. Then I explained that Françoise had had to go to Paris, but would be back very shortly. Unfortunately, I went on, I should have to leave myself within the next hour. Could she possibly come over and keep Mme Desnoyers company until Françoise returned? 'She is not well,' I added. Clearly this news had been kept from everybody, and I sat as patiently as I could while sympathy was being expressed. Was it this flu she had been reading about in the medical page of *Le Figaro*?

'I am not sure,' I lied. 'She is in bed. But I don't think she should be alone. If you could come over I know she would be pleased to see you.'

This, apparently, was not convenient. She was expecting a friend, though in this weather the friend, who was elderly and not in good health, might prefer not to go out. In fact she herself was feeling rather tired. 'I don't complain,' she said proudly, but it was not easy, living alone. Not that I knew anything about that, but one had to be so careful with one's health. Naturally . . .

Extreme tension gives one a certain authority, as I then discovered. 'Madame,' I said firmly. 'I should be obliged if you would take a taxi and come over here as soon as possible. I will then take the taxi on to Paris. When Françoise returns she will drive you home. I am sorry if this is inconvenient, but, as I say, it is a matter of urgency. I have a train to catch, and must be in London tonight.'

There were sounds of bewilderment, of hesitation. I persisted. I feel she should not be alone until Françoise arrives, I said. Clearly, as a mere visitor, I could not care for her. In any case she would be happy to see a member of her family; this was, after all, a family matter. It was only for a brief hour or so, I went on. I should not want to have it on my conscience. . . . Or on hers, I implied. And it was imperative that I catch my train. Urgent family business. I was sure she understood. And the taxi was an absolute necessity. Was there a firm in Sucy-en-Brie that she knew of?

Oh, yes. She used them all the time, not being a driver herself.

'I will settle the bill in Paris,' I said.

'You will have to pay for the return journey, you know. Are you sure that you can do that?'

'Of course. I shall expect you very shortly. I'm sure they will be very grateful. As, of course, I am.'

I replaced the receiver firmly and went next door to pay my last—my last ever—visit to Mme Desnoyers. She was sleeping almost naturally, and it occurred to me again that the sedatives Françoise had administered were, or had been, extremely strong. This was a matter I decided to leave undisturbed. If Mme Mercier was worried she would call a doctor. Humble people tend to be faithful: it is their great, their undervalued virtue. I smoothed the sheet, opened the window a little way to let in some air, and left as silently as I had entered. I knew I should not come back.

I went out to the drive to greet Mme Mercier, who emerged from the taxi looking uncertain. I smiled steadily and ushered her into the house. Before she could interrogate me, as she was entitled to do, I picked up my small bag and escaped to the haven of the taxi. There had been no explanation of my movements that would sound even halfway convincing. As the taxi moved off I realized that I was shaking. 'Paris,' I managed to say. '*Vous connaissez la rue Delambre?*' '*Oui, oui.*' He was a Parisian who had moved to Sucy to be near his daughter and son-in-law, but he missed the old place. He embarked on a cheerful monologue, to which I made a few responses. As we moved on to the main road I could see Françoise's car coming from the opposite direction. As it passed me I waved briefly, but made no other move. My days as a compliant accomplice were at an end.

18

WE HAD FAILED EACH OTHER; THAT MUCH WAS CLEAR.
But, interestingly, this was never referred to. Friendship sometimes demands less than full disclosure, and it may be more
comfortable to abstain from an accountability which may leave
one open to criticism. When I got back to the hotel I found
that my old room had been cleared of Françoise's belongings,
and took this as a sign that the incident was closed. I did not
expect to hear from her, nor did I until six months had elapsed,
when I received an invitation to her wedding to Jean-Charles.
I did not go, although I sent my very best wishes. But I did go
when their baby was born, and have visited fairly regularly
since. They invite me to spend part of my summer holiday
there, which is thoughtful of them, and we have found a way of
being friendly without the intimacy that formerly obtained
between Françoise and myself. This is a code to which we can
all conform, all three of us, and I have become a seasoned visitor, as they are now seasoned hosts.

They are the most devoted of parents, united perhaps by the rush of primal feeling that overwhelmed them when Jean-Marie was born. It is possible that neither of them had ever experienced anything so spontaneous, so instinctive before this event: it has made them dependent on each other in a way that could never have been predicted. They gaze at him wonderingly; he stares back with the lordly indifference to which his beauty entitles him. He occasionally consents to hold my hand, and then there are three rapt faces bending over him. He was five months old at my last visit and has succeeded in imposing his will on his attendants. There is no doubt who will be master here.

Mme Desnoyers has never seen her grandson. She made a partial recovery from her second stroke, but her speech and mobility remained affected, and it was thought best to install her in a nursing home run by nuns on the far side of Sucy, where Françoise visits her faithfully every Sunday. The expense is considerable, but there no longer seems to be any shortage of money. My sympathy appears to be wasted; Françoise assures me that Mme Desnoyers is perfectly happy there. This I doubt. I recognize it, though, as part of her duty to her husband, who always detested Mme Desnoyers, and while exhibiting every kind of concern is more than happy to have her out of the way.

Her old room is now given over to Mme de Lairac, who pays a stately visit from time to time. I take good care never to coincide with these visits, for there is no love lost between us. She considers me an inconvenient witness to Françoise's former behaviour, although this is now a feature of a time long past. She still manages to imply that without her resources, which are considerable, the whole enterprise would have foundered. Although I assume that Jean-Charles earns more than enough to maintain his house and his family, it is understood that more money will become available on Mme de Lairac's demise. This keeps everyone on their best behaviour.

The house is much more comfortable now. Fernand and Mariette never returned, not even to claim the month's wages that were due to them. They have been replaced by Nicole and Delphine, two ladies from Mauritius. They are polite and dignified, and provide excellent service. Their days off alternate, so that there is always someone in the house to look after Jean-Marie. He in his turn adores them, nestles happily into their arms, and when he does so I see a flicker of sadness in Françoise's expression, as if this is the first intimation that she may eventually lose her son to other women. But she is extremely disciplined, and never refers to her feelings, having perhaps learned that it is imprudent to do so, or that such feelings should be evaluated in a steady and sober manner, something she was not always willing to do.

My former love of the house has been similarly evaluated. I see its beauty now in classical terms, complete with reference to its inhabitants, who conform, as if in a play, to the components of classical design. I am allowed a freedom there which I am careful not to exploit. Mostly I sit on the terrace with a book, or wander through the surrounding countryside. My favourite view of the house is from the long approach, towards the façade, my favourite time the early evening, when its outlines are slightly blurred, and its whiteness dimmed. That is when it appears at its most magical, and although the proportions remain resolutely, squarely, classical, its appeal is softer, more romantic, as if more than one life might be contained there. Of this, however, there is no sign, for all are more than content with the parts that have been allotted to them, and may even be genuinely happy.

After such visits I am newly reconciled to my small flat. When my tenure at the hotel expired I did not renew it. I work from home now, and do not much enjoy my brief visits to Paris now that old friends are no longer there. In London I can count on Philip, whose attempted reconciliation with his wife did not, as they say, work out. This poor little phrase, which was all that he offered in the way of explanation, signified his re-entry into my life. We are careful with each other: no more intemperate outbursts on my part, no more self-interested reserve on his. We have discovered an affinity that may not have been there before, and for the time being are content with this. I am fully aware that changes may yet take place, that I may reflect on these matters, and decide, quite suddenly, that I desire something more, something ardent and unrealistic, rather as if I were Françoise, prepared, all that time ago, to seek her fortune elsewhere. But then I know that both she and I have passed the age, and the stage of life, that permits such fantasies, and realize, perhaps a little bleakly, that both of us have done quite well, and that it would be pure folly to go in search of more.

My book is finished. It will go to the typist, and then to the editor, and then I must face a future without it. Philip has suggested that I do a further degree, possibly in design, and then set up as an independent consultant in landscape gardening. But I know the kind of gardens that English people favour and do not appreciate them much. In any case I prefer my gardens deserted, on misty mornings, at unpopular times of the year, compelling in their silence and their secrecy. I do not sympathize with extraneous ornaments, still less with barbecues and teak chairs and tables. In this I recognize that France has left its mark on me, and I am thankful for this. My task now is to come to terms with irreconcilables, to try to harmonize the formality of the one with the cheerfulness of the other. This may not be easy. But then I shall have time to bring it into line or to abandon it altogether. Maybe others will take a hand, as they did long ago, before nature asserted itself. And then nature will take over, revealing what was merely adumbrated in the first place. I am more or less comfortable, more or less contented. Not everyone is born to fulfil an heroic role. The only realistic ambition is to live in the present. And sometimes, quite often in fact, this is more than enough to keep one busy. Time, which was once squandered, must now be given over to the actual, the possible, and perhaps to that evanescent hope of a good outcome which never deserts one, and which should never be abandoned.

ABOUT THE TYPE

This book was set in Bembo, a typeface based on
an old-style Roman face that was used for Cardinal
Bembo's tract *De Aetna* in 1495. Bembo was cut by Fran-
cisco Griffo in the early sixteenth century. The Lanston
Monotype Company of Philadelphia brought the well-
proportioned letterforms of Bembo to the United States
in the 1930s.